Lucifer's Cage

After Dark
Book 6

Sarah Bailey

Lucifer's Cage Copyright © 2019 by Sarah Bailey

Please note the setting for this book is the United Kingdom.
The spelling throughout is British English.

Cover Art by Christian Bentulan

Published by Twisted Tree Publications
Visit their website at www.twistedtreepublications.com
Email them at info@twistedtreepublications.com

Paperback ISBN: 978-1-9996169-5-3

For Sean
The most wonderous time traveller I know
Your unwavering support is a gift
Thank you for being you

Contents

Chapter One

The King of Hell decided he was having a bad morning. Scrap that. He was having a bad day. No. He was having a bad fucking year. Lucifer was done with all the bullshit. *Screw my brothers and screw my Father.* What was the point in him being down here any longer? Surely there were enough demons to take care of business. It was a joke. God was a fucking joke. All that prophetic shit he'd spouted was just part of his ridiculous plan to punish his son. To teach Azrael a lesson for siding with Lucifer in the war in Heaven.

Typical. It was just typical of his father. Always plotting. Always taking things too far. Just like when he cast Lucifer from Heaven. Forcing him to punish those souls who had sinned. Given the name: The Devil. Lucifer was no devil. He would always be an Archangel. The light bringer. The Morningstar. His father's favourite son. Humanity believed he was evil. He supposed he lived up to the name to an extent. Played his part. He was the king. The Lord of Hell.

He lay on his bed, cursing his father. He was sick to death of idiotic demon squabbles and his dukes constantly demanding things of him. Lucifer wanted out of Hell. He wanted out of his duties. Yet ever since he'd arrived back after his last jaunt on Earth, he'd been unable to leave. He knew it was his father's doing. He clearly didn't want his son causing trouble.

Cursing again, he rolled on his side. One day he'd teach his father a lesson.

One damn day!

There was something shimmering in the periphery of his vision. He turned, sitting up. A purple light which looked distinctly like a portal appeared in the ceiling of his bedroom.

What the fuck?

The next moment a girl with bright pink hair dropped out of it and crashed down on top of him. He grunted at the impact. Their limbs were a tangled mess on the bed.

"Ouch, what the hell?" she said, the tone of her voice having a singsong lilt to it.

She shifted on top of him, propping herself up by her hands. The girl stared down at him with wide violet eyes. There was confusion, fear and curiosity in her expression. She opened and closed her mouth like a fish. He eyed her with suspicion. What the fuck was this girl doing in Hell? More to the point, why was she lying on top of him on his bed?

"Excuse me," he said.

"Oh shit, I'm sorry!"

She was slow to get off him. He deftly caught her around the waist and reversed their positions, pinning her down with his body. He wanted answers. Girls didn't fall out of the ceiling from portals into Hell. Especially not in his private chambers.

"Who are you and what are you doing here?" he demanded.

"Who are you?" she retorted, staring up at him with those inscrutable violet eyes.

Her bright pink hair shimmered in the light, falling back on the bed. He noticed the slight curve of the tips of her ears. The girl below him was most definitely fae, but not full blooded. No, there was something else about her.

"The Devil, girl. Now, answer me."

Her mouth fell open on a gasp. His eyes were drawn to her full lips. Her body beneath his was warm. Her curves soft and delectable.

She did just fall into my bed. It has been a long time since I've touched a woman.

He'd been too busy to engage in such activities. His mind raced with dark thoughts about what lay beneath her clothes. There was no reason for him to be thinking these things. He shook himself internally.

Quit being the rogue everyone thinks you are, Lucifer.

"Candace... My name is Candace," she squeaked.

"And what are you doing in my bed, Candace?"

"I didn't mean to. Someone pushed me. I didn't know."

She was telling him the truth. He was sure of it. He wished his father hadn't taken away his ability to hear the thoughts of humans, but it wouldn't have mattered anyway. She wasn't all human as it was.

"Where am I?" she asked.

"Hell. In my private chambers."

"Are you really... Lucifer?"

His lips curved up at the sides.

"Yes."

Candace couldn't believe her eyes nor her ears. Lying on top of her, his body flush with hers, was the original fallen angel himself. She hadn't bargained on this when Jax had thrown her head first into a portal. How had she wound up in Hell of all places?

She stared up at the angel. His dark hair fell into his eyes. He was devastating on so many levels. He exuded power and danger. His dark, mesmerising eyes burnt holes into hers. Her skin thrummed with electricity from where he was pinning her hands down to the bed.

Holy fucking shit. The Devil himself is on top of me and all I can do is stare at him.

She needed to unstick her tongue from the roof of her mouth. Getting herself out of this awkward situation and back to Earth were her priorities. She was going to hunt down Jax and give him a piece of her mind.

Where the fuck does he get off pushing me into a portal to Hell?

"Can you maybe let me go?" she asked.

"You have not yet given me an adequate explanation for your presence."

She supposed she owed him something. *I did land on top of him.* Yet she didn't quite appreciate him holding her down. His body against hers was distracting in ways she didn't like to think about. Her heart thundered in her chest.

There was one way she could extract herself from this thoroughly compromising position. Pink smoke trickled from her fingertips. His eyes were drawn to it.

"Oh, dear girl, none of that," he said, freezing the smoke in place. "You have more than just fae magic. Interesting."

She almost cursed. She should've known he would be able to stop her from using her inheritance from her father. He was an angel. A devastatingly attractive angel, but an angel nonetheless.

"What are you?"

How could she explain such a thing?

"Well, you obviously know I'm half fae," she said.

"What else, girl?"

Not getting out of this one so easily I guess.

"Human..."

His eyebrow arched up. There was no point trying to lie to him.

"Witch. My father is a witch."

"That explains your little magic trick."

The smoke at her fingertips disappeared.

"Are you satisfied now?"

"Perhaps. Are you not enjoying this little interlude between us?"

The sultry look in his eyes sent a jolt down her spine. She wasn't about to admit anything of the sort to him. No matter that her body was responding to his in ways she was very uncomfortable with. She fought against the instinct to hook a leg around his and draw him closer.

"No."

He let go of one of her hands only to run his down her bare arm. He caught her face by her chin. Staring down at her with an intensity which made her tremble with anticipation, Lucifer was sure not one to hold anything back. She wasn't sure what else she'd expected.

"Your accelerated pulse speaks volumes, girl. I can see it in your eyes. Desire is a potent drug. One you should be careful not to get lost in. Did no one ever tell you it's dangerous to play games with the Devil?"

The words he'd said weren't the most distracting thing about the last thirty seconds. No. His soft skin on hers. That set everything on fire.

Desire doesn't quite cut it. What I'm feeling is unlike anything else I've ever experienced. Holy fuck. I need to get a grip.

She needed him off. Right now. Before she did something she regretted.

"I have no interest in playing any sort of game with you."

He smiled, his bottom lip caught between his teeth. It almost made her melt into a pool of jelly on the spot. He was right. Lusting after the Devil was the last thing she should be doing. There was only one other course of action she could resort to.

She gave him her brightest smile. His eyes narrowed. She delivered a swift knee to the groin which had him grunting and rolling off her. She scrambled off his bed, retreating behind the desk on the other side of his room.

He sat up a moment later, eyes blazing with unconcealed fury.

He left me with no choice, but shit, he looks so mad.

"I'm sorry," she said, putting her hands up. "I shouldn't have done that, but you wouldn't get off me."

He jumped up, stalking towards her. His hands slammed down on the desk as he reached it.

"I'm sorry," she repeated.

"Ask next time."

She dropped her hands, scowling. He was the one who hadn't moved even when she'd asked him the first time.

"I did. You were the one who insisted on pinning me down on your bed."

His expression turned devious, eyes roaming down the length of her in a distinctly predatory way. She swallowed, trying not to choke on her own breath.

"Mmm, yes, well... I haven't quite decided whether or not I want to do that again."

Excuse me? Did he just say what I think he did?

Her cheeks grew hot. This was not where she envisioned this conversation going.

Time to change the subject.

"So, um... this is Hell." She looked around at his room. "Not quite what I expected."

He arched a perfect black eyebrow.

"Did you think we lived in squalor down here?"

5

"No, of course not. I just thought it'd be more... you know... fiery."

He snorted, rolling his eyes.

"You forget, these are my private rooms. No fires. No punishment. I have no interest in dealing with that side of things. That doesn't change the fact that you should not be here."

There was no question about that. She hadn't wanted to be dropped into Hell, especially not right on top of Lucifer. She wondered what the rest of Hell looked like.

Lucifer's bedroom was relatively modern. His bed, which was huge, took up most of the back wall. His desk was black with chrome legs. The walls were midnight blue and there were several bookshelves lining them. His bedroom was more suited to an expensive penthouse in London than Hell.

She eyed him again. His hands were still flat on the desk, his dark eyes roaming across her. There was something about the angel which set her hair on end. Goose pimples rose on her arms. She wished he'd stop looking at her like that. As if he wanted to devour her whole. There was no way she would ever let him get near enough to her again to do such a thing. Absolutely no way. Not even the memory of his skin on hers would shake her resolve. She shivered at the thought.

Nope. I don't want him touching me again. Nope. Not at all. Even if it felt deliciously wonderful. Nope. Get a damn grip! He is dangerous.

"Don't get me wrong, I know I shouldn't be here. It's just I can't create portals, so you know, I might need some help returning to Earth."

She didn't want to ask him for anything, but she had little choice in the matter. The Devil was her only way out of here as far as she could tell. She wasn't about to go wandering around Hell to find another way.

He was silent for several long moments, staring at her with an unreadable expression.

"There's one little issue with that," he said, straightening and looking down at his nails.

"And what would that be?"

Wasn't he going to help her? She wasn't sure why she was surprised. He was the Devil after all. He didn't seem like the type to offer his assistance to anyone.

6

"You see, someone changed the rules in Hell after a little incident on Earth last year."

"The rules? What incident?"

What is he talking about?

She hadn't heard of anything happening recently, but she tended to stay out of supernatural politics. It was bad enough being dragged into witch business given who her father was.

"Not up to date with the end of the world news? Hmm, well, never mind. It is hardly relevant now. No, you see, our ever-illustrious creator decided no one gets out of Hell any more. I'm afraid you bagged yourself a one-way ticket here."

Chapter Two

Candace stared at Lucifer for what seemed like eternity. What did he mean she couldn't return to Earth? Demons had free reign up there. She'd met more than enough in her short twenty-four years.

"Are you seriously telling me I'm stuck here?"

"For the time being, yes."

Her legs almost buckled. She slumped down in his desk chair, putting her head in her hands.

"Fuck."

Stuck in Hell. How had this happened? She really was going to kill Jax. How could he do this to her? Unless he hadn't known. But it was Jax. He always knew what he was doing.

She raised her head, looking up at Lucifer with wide eyes. His expression was neutral.

"But I'm not supposed to be here," she said.

"That can't be helped now. No one is leaving any time soon."

"Not even you?"

He rolled his eyes, clicking his tongue.

"No, not even me. I might be an angel but even I have to answer to God's Will."

"You're telling me the only person who can fix this is God himself?"

"Perhaps. Perhaps not."

Cryptic much?

How was she going to get out of here? When she'd gone to deal with a feud between a witch and a fae, she did not expect to encounter her best friend there. It had escalated way beyond her control. She supposed that's what she got when her father insisted she be an emissary to the fae. Being half witch made her relationship with them difficult.

"Well, fine. What are you going to do with me then?"

It was a pertinent question. She didn't fancy seeing more of Hell than she had to. Would he hand her off into the care of one of his demons?

"It would not do to have you roaming around getting into trouble."

"Who said I would get into trouble?"

"Would you like me to toss you into the viper's nest, so you can find out?"

"No, but what are you going to do?"

He grinned, eyes twinkling with mischief.

"The options are endless, but I imagine you don't wish your stay here to involve any sort of punishment."

Punishment from demons? No way. But the thought of punishment from him sent her pulse into overdrive.

Nope. Nope. Nope. Not going there.

"No."

"You'll just have to stay right here." His eyes raked across her chest. "With me."

She spluttered. With him? Was he for real right now? There was no way she wanted to spend her time in Hell with the sinfully attractive Devil.

Absolutely not. Under no circumstances can I be in the same room as him for the foreseeable future. How can I when he looks at me like that?

His dark eyes were magnetic, roaming across her with unconcealed admiration.

"You're not serious."

"Where else would you like me to put you?"

He walked around the desk with slow, measured steps. If she had any willpower, she would've got up and moved as far away from him as possible. He tucked a finger under her chin, forcing her to look up at him.

"You see, Candace, there is no safer place in Hell than with me, the King."

Here with Lucifer was most definitely not the safest place she could be. She slapped his hand away, scowling.

"You say that like you're some kind of fucking knight in shining armour, which, I might add, you are most decidedly not."

He smirked.

"Hmm, perhaps not, but you don't have a choice in the matter. Don't forget, this is my domain. What I say goes."

She hadn't forgotten. Crossing her arms over her chest, she let out a breath.

"Fine, just keep your hands to yourself."

That made his eyes widen a fraction, but his smirk remained, and he was still standing far too close to her.

"Are you sure about that?"

"Perfectly."

She stood up. Their bodies were inches apart. She craned her neck up to look at the tall angel. Heat radiated from him. It was hard to think straight, but she was determined not to allow him to gain the upper hand.

"Don't test me, Lucifer," she said. "I'm not a plaything for your amusement."

He reached up. His hand hovered over her hair for a moment before he twirled the strands around his fingers. Her breath caught in her throat. Her bright pink hair was just the latest in a long line of outlandish colours she chose deliberately to irritate her father.

"Half fae and yet I do not believe this is what it looks like naturally," he said, his voice low.

"No," she replied.

"Will you tell me?"

His voice took on a seductive note to it.

Fuck my life. Why? Why is he so goddamn alluring?

"No."

Ever since she was a child, her father had insisted she kept it secret. The fae could change their hair colour at will. It was a gift she'd inherited.

"Why ever not?"

"What makes you think it's any of your business?"

His hand curled around the back of her head, his thumb brushing along her cheek.

"It isn't, but you're going to tell me. Maybe not now, but one day."

He released her abruptly, turning away and striding towards the double doors a few feet away from them. He waved a hand at her, indicating she should follow him. The only problem was she felt rooted to the spot, completely undone by that simple touch. She put a hand to her cheek, knowing her face was burning.

"Come along. If you're going to stay here, then I suppose I shall give you the grand tour."

She unstuck her feet from the floor and trudged along after him, feeling as though she was in for one heck of a bumpy ride.

Sat on his throne, Lucifer drummed his fingers on the armrest. There were several issues requiring his attention, but he couldn't concentrate properly. His mind rested firmly on the girl he'd left in his private chambers. The half witch, half fae girl who barrelled her way into his life like a fucking thunderstorm.

Time did not pass in the same way in Hell as it did up on Earth, but at an estimate, it had been at least a week since she'd landed on top of him. A week of pure torture. There was a part of him that wanted to pin her down on his bed and fuck her senseless. The memory of her supple, curvaceous body beneath his assaulted all his senses. His hand curled into a fist. The other half knew better than to get tangled up with a girl who shouldn't even be in Hell in the first place.

"My Lord?"

He looked up. His assistant, Mallmomoz, was staring at him with wide eyes.

"What?" he snapped.

"I said Dantalion is waiting."

Mall was just another in a long line of assistants, but she was one of the more competent demons. She didn't mince words, unlike the others. It was refreshing, but he had little patience for anyone these days.

"For fuck's sake. Does he ever not have something to complain about?"

She shrugged, handing him a report.

"It seems he is having a disagreement with Beleth again."

He looked down at the document, eyes scanning over the contents. He rolled his eyes, waving a hand at Mall.

"Fucking idiots. Fine, send him in. The sooner I get this over with, the better."

Mall disappeared for a moment. Lucifer stared down at his clenched fist.

How has she gotten under my skin in such a short space of time?

Maddening. The temptation to have her was absolutely maddening.

He knew she wasn't immune to him by any stretch of the imagination despite what she might say. If only he didn't have to deal with this ridiculous situation, he could go back and see her. Maybe she'd give into him. He hadn't yet broached the subject with her since that first day. She was sullen and uncommunicative for the first few days. He supposed he could hardly blame her. He was just as irritated being stuck down here unable to leave when he pleased. His father had taken away his freedom yet again.

There was a commotion outside his throne room. Two demons burst through the doorway, Mall hot on their heels.

"I told you this is my meeting," Dantalion shouted.

"I don't give a shit. This has gone on long enough," Beleth retorted.

Lucifer wanted to put his head in his hands.

Great. Just fucking great. Both of them at the same time.

The two of them didn't pay him any mind, both arguing at the top of their voices.

"Enough. Would you two pipe the fuck down for one minute?" he said, his voice carrying across the room.

Dantalion, Beleth and Mall froze, all turning his way. He hadn't moved from his throne, but Lucifer's expression was thunderous. As if his day wasn't already shaping up to be a nightmare, he had to deal with his two most argumentative and disruptive dukes.

Beleth had gotten worse since he'd been confronted by Michael during the fight against the Darkness. Lucifer rolled his eyes. He hadn't been bothered when he'd discovered his demons were colluding with angels and creating hybrids. Michael orchestrating the entire plan changed things.

The self-righteous prick.

He wasn't as innocent as he liked to think. Involving humans in their schemes. Lucifer never thought he'd see the day when his brothers and sisters would stoop to such levels.

"My Lord," Dantalion said, bowing. "I specifically requested this meeting without his presence."

Dantalion sent a glare Beleth's way. The other demon just scoffed.

"You think our Lord gives a shit about that. We have more important things to be concerned about than your petty vendetta against me," Beleth said.

If Lucifer let this go on, there would be no stopping either of them from exploding into a full-blown row. Then he'd never be able to leave his throne room.

"I said enough. Beleth, stop antagonising him and leave his territory alone. I am done listening to the two of you squabble. Get your shit together. Do you really think I have time for your antics?"

There was silence for several moments. Dantalion crossed his arms over his chest, still glaring at Beleth. Steam rose from his nostrils.

"Understood, my Lord," Beleth said before he bowed. "I apologise for Dantalion wasting your time."

"Both of you are. This is the last time. If I hear about this again, I will not hesitate to strip you both of your titles and throw you to the wolves. Am I making myself clear?"

The two demons nodded, both scowling. Lucifer knew it was not the last time he would hear from them, but right now, he couldn't care less. He wanted them out of here.

Beleth stepped forward.

"My Lord, there is a much more serious matter at hand. We are still unable to return to Earth. You said this would not go on long."

He should've known this would come up. He drummed his fingers on the arm of his throne again, eyes falling on Mall. She strode over to him, standing by his side and turning to Dantalion and Beleth.

"Our Lord is dealing with the matter. It is not quite as simple as we first imagined," she said.

"Our Lord is taking his sweet time," Beleth retorted.

Lucifer flattened his hand, gripping the arm. Mall glanced at him for a moment before levelling her gaze on the other demons again.

"You would do well to watch your tongue, Beleth. You answer to Lucifer, not the other way around."

"You are aware I wish to retrieve my daughter and her lover from Earth. Their combined power would be an asset to us."

Lucifer stood up abruptly. He held back from outright growling at Beleth, but his patience was shot. If Beleth tried such a thing, he would bring Michael down on their heads. He was in no mood to deal with his brother.

"You will not go after your daughter or her partner. They are under Finnegan's charge and it will remain that way. My word on this is final. As for the other matter, it is being dealt with. You are both dismissed."

He strode from the room, ignoring the anger on Beleth's face.

He can just fucking well deal with it. And if he doesn't, I'll just put him in his place.

He stood in the hallway for a moment, his hand planted on the wall. White-hot rage consumed him. If his father hadn't trapped them all down here, his demons wouldn't be so restless. But fuck, if he wasn't the most restless and irritable of them all.

He stalked down the hallway, pushing open the double doors at the end. He faltered on the threshold. Candace was sprawled out on his bed, the covers twisted around her. He could see her luscious rear peeking out, clad in only black, lacy underwear, her bare legs on show. He became hyper aware of his instant reaction to her state of undress.

Fuck. Fuck. Fuck.

Chapter Three

ucifer clenched and unclenched his fists several times. All his anger evaporated only to be replaced by the raging flame of desire.

I could've sworn I made sure she had appropriate clothing for this. Why is she half naked in my bed? That girl, this little witch. How is this fair?

His feet carried him towards her. If he could just get his insatiable lust under control for one moment, but there was no stopping the burning need inside him. He had to have this girl.

When he reached the bed, he hesitated. She was fast asleep. Her pink hair spread out across the pillow, half tangled over her face. He leant over and brushed it away. Her brow was furrowed, eyes darting around under her eyelids.

He stilled. What was he doing? Behaving as though he was some baseless human, controlled by emotions, desires. Reminded that he'd once chastised Azrael for his feelings for Alice, the girl sent to destroy the world.

He would not stoop to such a level no matter how tempting the prospect of fucking her might be. Holding her down and showing her no mercy. Hearing her scream his name whilst he took her with ruthless abandon. He would ruin her for anyone else. Ruin this girl so she couldn't do anything but come crawling back to him for more. And he would give it to her, over and over again.

He reached out and untangled the covers from her legs, settling them over her. If he gave in, it would be more trouble than it was worth. He had enough on his plate already. Besides, she could barely tolerate him being around.

Turning, he strode away and threw himself into his desk chair. There were a thousand things he should be doing right now. Fucking Candace senseless was not one of them.

He booted up his laptop. Modern technological advances had filtered their way down into Hell. It was high time he continued with his research.

His eyes kept finding her no matter how hard he tried to concentrate. She shifted, throwing the covers off. He could see the steady rise and fall of her chest, her legs spread wide. His eyes roamed lower, mouth going very dry when they landed on her inner thighs. A new wave of intense burning desire drove through him. He resisted the urge to slam his hand down on the desk.

He was about to get up and give into his need when she opened her eyes. Their gazes locked, her violet eyes wide with shock and confusion. There was no doubt she could see the intense longing in his own.

She looked down at herself. Scrambling to sitting position, she pulled the covers back over her legs. He rose very slowly, still staring at her.

"Lucifer..."

He stalked towards her.

"Don't," she whispered.

Ignoring her request, he knelt on the bed and crawled over her, forcing her to lie back down. Their bodies weren't touching. He could feel her trembling all the same.

"I warned you, Candace. I warned you playing games with me is dangerous."

"I wasn't playing a game. I was sleeping."

He cocked an eyebrow, leaning down until their breath mingled. He wasn't going to touch her. Yet.

"Are you sure that's appropriate sleepwear?"

She turned her face away. It made him grin.

She can't hide how much I affect her. I can feel her heart hammering in her chest. Her body screaming out for me. She wants me. This little witch wants me. I know she does.

"It's hot."

"It is Hell, girl."

He caught her face, turning it back towards him. Staring down at her mouth, he couldn't help but want to taste what she had to offer. But if he kissed her now, he wasn't sure he could stop at just that.

"Why do you care what I'm wearing?"

There was a very good reason why he cared. He nudged her legs open, so he could show her. It was a mistake. As soon as he pressed himself against her, he could feel her supple curves beneath the covers. It made him ache with longing. He wanted to tear away the rest of the barriers between them.

Her eyes widened to saucers, mouth opening on a quiet gasp.

"Does this tell you everything you need to know?" he asked, his voice a little hoarse.

"Yes," she whispered.

He could feel the heat between her legs. Shifting ever so slightly brought a quiet hiss from her lips. The ache grew. He needed to have her. To feel her writhing beneath him whilst he took her to the highest of highs. Candace would be his undoing if he wasn't careful.

"I told you, I'm not your plaything," she said, her voice taking on a high pitch note to it.

"Mmm, I'm not playing games. I think you know what I want."

She bit her lip. Was she going to give into him? Her expression hardened.

"Get off me, Lucifer. Now."

His smile grew.

I've flustered her and now she wants to take back control. Pity.

Her mouth was still so close, but he moved lower, his lips brushing along her bare collarbone. Her skin was soft. She shifted beneath him, her hands gripping the sheets. He continued his path down towards where the tops of her breasts were peeking out above her camisole. He paused. Their eyes met again. Her lips were parted, breath coming faster.

"Do you want me to stop?" he asked.

"Yes."

"I don't believe you."

Her hand came up, hovering above his head. He gave her a slow smile. She was teetering on the edge of something. He pressed his mouth to her skin again, just above her left breast. Another kiss. And another.

Her hand came down, tangling in his hair as she arched against him.

There we go, Candace. Now the truth of what you want comes to light.

"Fuck you," she whispered.

"I'd much rather fuck you," he replied, his voice just as low.

"I'm not going to let you do that."

"Perhaps not now, but soon, I'll have you. You won't be able to deny me."

Fingers dug into his hair. She pulled his head back, glaring at him.

"Never, Lucifer. I will never let you touch me like this again."

"You seem very sure about that."

"Just get off me. This might be your domain, but this is my body. You are not welcome to it."

Reaching up, he untangled her hand from his hair before pinning it to the bed.

"Mmm, you're only making it worse for yourself. That desire you feel is going to consume you. Mark my words, you'll come to me when you're ready and you'll come willingly."

He released her before she could answer him, rolling away and getting up off the bed. He didn't look at her as he stalked from the room. He knew she was probably cursing his back, but he didn't care. It was a battle of wills between them. There was every chance this would backfire spectacularly in his face, but now he'd felt her again. Felt every inch of her body pressed against his through the covers and their clothes.

There was no question any longer.

He would have that girl naked beneath him.

He would ruin her completely.

Candace's heart raced out of control. Her breathing completely erratic. All her thoughts were centred on where his mouth had been pressed up against her skin. She'd almost given in. Almost allowed him to take her under and drown her. She was sure if she let him touch her, taste her, fuck her, she wouldn't ever be able to come back from it.

Fuck you, Lucifer. Fuck you for making me so weak. For making me want you.

It was the first time he'd come near her since the day she'd arrived here. She'd been suspicious of his intentions towards her, but now she knew for certain. Lucifer wanted to possess her. And she was completely undone by their encounter with each other. How could she have allowed him near her again?

She knew Lucifer was trouble and staying with him was a mistake, but the thought of seeing more of Hell terrified her. She didn't want to know what happened to souls down here nor meet any demons.

Hating that he was right. Hating that she was probably safer with him than anyone else, she shifted, tearing the covers off her. She was hot and bothered. Her thighs were damp from her arousal drenching right through her underwear.

Why does he make me feel this way? He barely did anything to me. And then he just left.

Left her trying to swim against the current of their mutual attraction. She slammed her fist down on the bed, a growl of frustration tearing from her lips.

"You will be the fucking death of me, Lucifer, I swear to fucking god. You are the most sinfully attractive man I've ever met and yet I can't have you under any circumstances."

And now she was talking to herself.

Just fucking great.

She got up, striding into the bathroom just off his bedroom. There was no lock on the door, but he'd not tried anything. Yet.

Not caring at that moment, she stripped off her clothes and jumped in the shower, setting it to cold. She shivered underneath the stream of water, wincing at the temperature, but it was needed. Anything to cool the flame burning inside her.

When she was done, she hot footed it into the walk-in wardrobe on the other side of his bedroom. He'd cleared a space and given her clothes. She could only be glad they weren't revealing. It seemed he'd made a judgement from what she'd been wearing when she'd fallen through the portal. She preferred practicality.

Selecting a pair of black jeans along with a red and black chequered shirt, she pulled on a pair of socks and calf high black boots. When she looked in the mirror, she realised her hair looked very much out of place with her current ensemble. Whilst she'd never go back to her natural colour, there were a myriad of different shades she could choose from.

She was pleased with her selection as she braided her hair down one side of her head. Her stomach growled.

Food. I most definitely need food.

She strode out of the wardrobe, through his bedroom and into his large living area.

Lucifer was sprawled out on the sofa, his arm thrown across his face. She ignored him, going straight towards the kitchen. He might not need to eat, but she did. She'd been living off a diet of instant noodles and cereal whilst she'd been down here. She couldn't cook. She burnt toast every time she tried to make it.

Back on Earth, her flat was filled with ready meals and takeaway boxes. She knew it was bad for her, but she was too busy with witch business and the fae to worry too much about her eating habits.

"Have I not given you enough choice, Candace? Why is it that I always seem to find empty packets of noodles lying around?" came a voice from the sofa.

She jumped, turning and glaring at him. He hadn't moved from his spot. Why did he care?

"I can't cook anything else, okay?"

It was a little embarrassing to admit. He sat up, his mesmerising eyes landing squarely on hers.

"You can't cook?"

"No... My father tried to teach me, but I'm useless."

The smirk which appeared on his lips irritated her. He rose, walking over and stopping on the other side of the breakfast bar.

"Oh well, you should've said."

He waved a hand and a plate appeared in front of him. A full English breakfast. A mug of tea sat steaming beside it. Her mouth fell open.

"How did you...?"

"I may be known as the Devil, but I am still an Archangel. There are many things I can do. You will inform me when you require feeding from now on."

His tone brokered no objection. He pulled out the stool and indicated she should sit down. She made her way around the counter, hesitating as she reached the stool. His hand was resting on the back of it. He was much too close to her. Her pulse spiked.

Damn it. I want him. I want him so much it fucking burns.

"Sit down before it gets cold."

She slid onto the stool, picking up the knife and fork. He leant over her, his mouth closed to her ear. His fingers brushed over the back of her neck, before he gripped her braid. Her breath caught in her throat. What was he doing?

"I like your hair this way."

She hadn't really thought about what his reaction to her changing her hair colour might be. She'd chosen a mixture of red, orange and yellow in subtle tones blending into one another.

"It's like a fire, the flames threatening to consume you. It's very fitting, don't you think?"

She could barely think of a suitable response to that.

"Keep it like this, Candace. Keep it this way whilst you're burning, aching for me to take you."

He released her braid, running his fingers down her neck again.

"I'll know when you've given in."

He walked away. She sat there, staring down at her plate of food, fighting the urge to chase after him. She wanted his hands on her again. She wanted to feel Lucifer everywhere.

And she was well and truly screwed now.

He'd stoked the flames and she was burning.

Burning for him like her flaming hair.

Fuck you, Lucifer. Fuck you.

Chapter Four

Candace strolled into the living room a few days later, looking for Lucifer. She stopped dead in her tracks. Standing in the middle of the room was a blonde woman with her hair in a tight ponytail. She was in come fuck me heels, a tight black skirt and a white shirt. She had a tablet in her hands.

They stared at each other.

Who the fuck is this? Why is she in Lucifer's private rooms and why the fuck does she look like sex on legs? Is he fucking this woman? Is that why she's wearing such provocative clothing?

Anger flooded her senses. No. She realised it wasn't anger. It was jealousy. How could she be jealous? Lucifer didn't mean anything to her.

"Hello," the woman said. "You must be my Lord's guest."

Candace almost choked on her own breath. *Her Lord? What?* Was she talking about Lucifer?

"Who are you?"

"Mallmomoz, but you may call me Mall."

Candace folded her arms across her chest, levelling the woman with a questioning stare.

"What exactly did he say about me?"

"My Lord informed me he had a guest. I have strict instructions not to allow anyone else access to his rooms."

She supposed as the King of Hell, he would require his subjects to refer to him as such.

"And what is it that you do for Lucifer?"

Mall smiled at her, shaking her head a little.

"I assist him in running his domain. I suppose you could refer to me as his personal assistant. Oh, he left you a note on the counter over there."

Mall pointed to the breakfast bar. Candace didn't move. This was his assistant. Did that mean she wasn't some kind of sexual plaything for him? Why would she even think that Lucifer had one of those in the first place? Mall didn't look much like a demon.

"Would it be rude of me to ask what exactly you are?" Candace said.

"A succubus, but do not worry, my duty is to my Lord. You are his guest, and as such, you are not to be harmed under any circumstances."

She let out the breath she was holding. If Mall was a succubus, it explained why she looked the way she did. She took slow steps towards the breakfast bar, interested in why Lucifer had left her a note.

I have left you something in the fridge. 2 minutes in the microwave, no longer.

She opened the fridge and sure enough, there was a plate inside covered by a plastic lid. She didn't even look under it as she shoved it in the microwave. She was hungry. It's why she'd been looking for him in the first place. She hadn't eaten so well in years.

"Um, so... where is he?" she asked Mall whilst she waited.

"In the throne room. He didn't wish to wake you. He asked me to retrieve something for him and to check if you had eaten."

Lucifer being considerate was something new on her.

The microwave dinged. She pulled out the plate and took off the lid. It was a simple pasta dish, but she appreciated it nonetheless. Grabbing a glass of water, she sat down at the breakfast bar and tucked in.

"You can tell him I have," she said between mouthfuls.

"You are not what I expected."

Candace turned, looking at Mall with confusion.

"When my Lord informed me of your presence, he did not say much about you. Only that you had accidentally arrived in Hell and whilst we are unable to return to Earth, you would be under his protection."

"Does he not have guests then?"

"Not often, no."

She turned back to her plate. She felt like she'd just learnt a great deal about the King of Hell in the last five minutes.

"How long have you been his assistant?"

"We do not measure time here, but I suppose around four hundred human years."

Candace almost spat out her food. Four hundred years? Then she remembered. Lucifer was the original fallen angel.

He's immortal, you big idiot.

"Will you tell me more about him?"

She wasn't quite sure why she'd asked that.

"I'm not sure I should be talking about him and I really must get back."

"I'm sorry, I shouldn't have... Forget I said anything."

She stared down at her almost empty plate. She hadn't realised she'd eaten it so fast. The stool next to her was pulled back. Mall sat down and turned to her, placing her tablet down on the counter.

"My Lord has been irritable for months since he returned to Earth. I worry we will not find a way to reverse what He has done to Hell."

"You mean the whole being stuck down here thing."

"Yes, but since you arrived, he's been worse. He paces the throne room with a restlessness I have never seen before. He usually spends most of his time in here, but it seems that with you around, he is less inclined to return to his rooms."

Candace knew very well why that was. Whilst he'd been making sure she ate well, he barely spent any more time than he had to around her. She could see the longing, desire in his eyes whenever they were together in the same room. It made it difficult to focus on anything but him.

I can't. I just can't. It wouldn't be right. He's the Devil.

There were a million reasons why she couldn't let him take her, but all of them seemed to disappear out of her head whenever he was near.

"Um, well... we don't exactly see eye to eye."

"And yet he protects you all the same."

Candace shrugged. She wasn't about to tell Mall that Lucifer was only doing this because he wanted to fuck her. The thought of it brought heat to her cheeks.

"Tell me, what do you do back on Earth?" Mall said.

"Oh well, I'm emissary to the fae. You see, I'm only a half blood. My father is a witch. I attend to his affairs in London."

"Interesting."

By the time Lucifer arrived back, Mall and Candace had been chatting for what seemed like forever. She felt it the moment he entered the room. Everything centred on that damn angel when he was near her.

"Mall," Lucifer said, his voice cold. "I have been waiting for you."

Mall stood, bowing to him.

"I apologise my Lord. Your lady friend wanted some company."

His eyes narrowed, falling on Candace. The hairs on the back of her neck stood to attention.

"Well, I suppose I have been neglecting my guest of late."

Mall bowed again, giving Candace a little wave before she slipped from the room. Lucifer waved a hand and the plate in front of her disappeared. She'd long finished her meal anyway.

She stood up, facing him.

"Don't be mad at Mall," she blurted out. "I was asking her questions about Hell. I'm sorry I kept her away."

His mesmerising eyes raked across her, taking in every inch of her body before falling on her hair. She hadn't changed the colour. There was no way she could after what he'd said. She always matched her hair to her outfits, but now, she had no choice but to deal with it.

"If I had known you lacked for company, I would've asked her to stop in with you sooner."

"Is she the only one who knows I'm here?"

"Yes."

"Why?"

He took several steps forward but came to a halt a few feet away from her. Even from this distance, he was too close. Her body thrummed.

"Do you realise how it would look to my demons? Protecting a girl from Earth for no good reason."

"I never asked you to protect me."

"And yet, you've never thanked me for it either."

He had a point. It would look bad if they knew she was staying here with him.

"Thank you."

"Was that really so hard?"

She wanted to throw something at his head. Why did he have to be so obnoxious and sarcastic? She was trying to be civil and polite. It wouldn't do to engage in a battle of words with him again.

"No, but I still don't understand..."

He arched an eyebrow. How could she finish that sentence? She'd been about to tell him she didn't understand why they couldn't stay away from each other. Why every time she looked at him, her whole world flipped on its axis and all she wanted was to drown in him.

"Understand what?"

She took a step towards him.

"This," she whispered.

"This?"

"You. Me. This."

Why the hell did I just say that? I'm such an idiot.

He smiled a little, but it was a sad smile.

"Why are you doing this? Why me? What do you have to gain from protecting me?"

"Who said I had anything to gain from it?"

It was his turn to take a step towards her.

"You don't seem like the type to do anything for anyone else unless it's of benefit to you."

"You have a low opinion of me."

"You've done nothing but live up to your reputation."

"Have I not taken care of you? Is that the type of thing the Devil would do?"

That brought her up short. She stepped back, suddenly finding it hard to breathe. His very presence suffocated her. Heat pooled everywhere. His eyes darkened further as if they weren't already almost black as it was.

"As to why I am doing this... I thought you'd have understood by now. Did I not make myself clear?"

He advanced on her. She backed away until she felt the counter behind her. She had nowhere left to go. He rested his hands either side of her, I caging her in.

"Tell me, Candace, would you like to be treated as one of my subjects?"

"No," she whispered.

"No? So, you do want me to treat you like you're my guest."

"Yes."

"I think you want more than that from me."

Fuck him. I hate him so much, but I want him all the same.

Her chest felt tight. She clenched her legs together, trying to stem the raging tide of her desire. He was much too close. All her senses went into overdrive. She needed this man. Needed him to tear off her clothes and fuck her with ruthless abandon. It's what she wanted.

There was no point in denying it to herself.

But admitting such a thing to him?

Impossible.

"You don't know anything about me."

"Oh, I know plenty about you. Candace Cadmi Highmore, daughter of Gallian Highmore, head of the Grand Coven."

She went deadly still. He knew who her father was. How did he know? She hadn't told him. He reached up, tucking her hair behind her ear.

"Did you think I wouldn't discover your true identity? I am the King of Hell, girl. You should know better. Quite the scandal your father caused, bringing home a half fae daughter and yet no one knows who gave birth to you."

"He didn't tell me."

His hand cupped the back of her neck, forcing her to look at him.

"You're lying to me. Who is your mother?"

"What makes you think I'd tell you anything?"

He gripped her neck tighter. She tried not to wince.

"You're far too stubborn."

"You might know who my father is, but you still don't know a thing about me."

She reached up, grabbing his hand and pulling it away from her neck. She held it between them.

"Is this why you're denying me? Because your father wouldn't approve?"

"You can look up all the information about me you want, that doesn't change anything between us. Of course, he wouldn't approve if he found out, but that's the thing, he doesn't approve of anything I do. I am his biggest disappointment. No matter how hard I try to live up to his standards."

His eyes widened a fraction. She didn't let go of his hand despite the electricity sparking up her arm.

"If you'd bothered to ask me about him, to ask me anything about myself, then perhaps I would've told you. You just want me for one thing and one thing alone. And that's exactly why this will never happen."

They stared at each other for the longest time. It was now or never.

"You want to know the real reason I won't let you fuck me like you want to," she whispered. "Because you don't care about me. You'll break me, Lucifer, and I'll never come back from it. You'll get to walk away from me, but I'll never be able to walk away from you. That's why I can't do this with you. Not now. Not ever."

Chapter Five

*L*ucifer took a step back as if she'd slapped him, breaking the contact between them. She took the opportunity to slip away from him, retreating towards the door to his bedroom. She turned back. He was still staring at the counter where she'd been moments before.

"If you had any consideration at all, you'd stop pursuing me," she said.

His head snapped up. His eyes were blazing with emotions she didn't understand. He strode towards her, gripping her arm in an iron hold when he reached her.

"Do you think you get to just leave after saying something like that?" he said, his voice brimming with barely contained rage.

"Oh, like you don't fucking walk away every damn time we talk to each other!"

"Do you think I want to? I am not an animal who cannot control himself and yet you, you drive me fucking crazy. You'd never forgive me if I took what I wanted without your consent so don't you fucking put that shit on me."

The wild look in his eyes had her heart hammering out of control.

I drive him crazy? He drives me fucking crazy too.

Before she really knew what she was doing, she'd closed the distance between them. Her mouth was so close to his. She could feel his harsh breath on her face.

"You dare try to take anything from me, I won't hesitate to use everything at my disposal to ensure you never come near me again," she hissed.

"Your magic won't save you from me. Nothing will. Don't forget who you're dealing with."

She could never forget who he was. The anger coursing through her was tangled up with lust.

Fuck my life. Lucifer, you're fucking killing me. I need you. I need everything about you.

"Do your fucking worst. I dare you."

The smirk which appeared on his lips enraged her further.

"If you want me, you know how to tell me."

Fuck you.

"Not happening."

"Then why is your mouth within an inch of mine? Do you want me to kiss you?"

She didn't have an answer for that.

I do. I want you to drown me.

"Fuck you," she whispered.

She wrenched her arm out of his grasp and strode away, slamming the door behind her. That man made her lose all sense of control. Why did he have to push her buttons? Her heart raced out of control. Her breathing was erratic.

"Fuck. Fuck. Fuck, you drive me nuts."

She wanted to scream. Frustration tore at her. Her entire body craved him and yet she wanted to punch his lights out.

What the fuck is wrong with me?

The door behind her slammed back on its hinges. She barely had a chance to turn around before he was backing her up against the bookcase by the wall.

"Tell me no," he said, his tone harsh. "Say it, Candace."

She stared up into his dark, mesmerising eyes. The ones which burnt holes into her soul. Fury, desire and lust emanated from him in waves.

"I can't," she whispered.

His mouth crashed down on hers with fierce brutality. His hands fisted in her hair, holding her in place whilst he devoured her whole.

Holy fuck.

She was kissing him back with as much ferocity. She gripped the front of his shirt, pulling him closer. She really was drowning. His kiss, electrifying. All rational thought flew from her head.

I want you. I want you so much it hurts.

"Let me have you. Give in to me."

The sudden intrusion of his thoughts into her head made her freeze. She shoved him back, breaking off their kiss.

"What the fuck?" she said.

He looked just as bewildered as she did. How had he heard her and she him? This was the last thing she needed. Him reading her mind. Yet did it really matter when he was staring at her like that? He was panting as hard as she was. And that kiss. That kiss just lit a fuse which set the whole damn world on fire.

She launched herself at him, hands tangling in his hair. If she had any willpower left to hold back, she would've, but it was shot to pieces the moment his mouth landed on hers.

Their second kiss was just as brutal as the first. She pushed him until he was backed up against his desk. He gripped her behind, pressing her into him. She could feel him everywhere and it was more than she could cope with. Everything felt like it was centred on their bodies fused together.

How the hell can you hear me?

"I don't know. He took that ability from me when he cast me from Heaven."

Have you heard me before?

"No. Only now."

She was rendered incapable of asking any further questions. He bit down on her bottom lip so hard, he drew blood. She cried out, wrenching away from him.

"What the hell? Where the fuck do you get off biting me?"

His eyes were like pools of never-ending darkness. The smile on his face made her blood pound in her ears. He tugged her back towards him and shoved his tongue in her mouth. She pushed at his chest, trying to get away from him, but he wouldn't budge. She could taste her own blood. It coated both of their mouths.

Stop. Stop it. Let me go.

He released her mouth, but his arms were still around her, keeping her body pressed to his.

"That was for making me wait," he said, his eyes glittering.

He was absolutely maddening.

"I fucking hate you," she hissed.

"Hate is such a strong word, don't you think?"

"Let me go. Now."

He dropped his arms. She took a step back, panting. Anger and desire coursed through her veins like wildfire. Letting him kiss her was a huge mistake. Kissing him back an even bigger one.

What the fuck am I doing?

The amusement in his expression made her rage burn hotter.

"I hope you're fucking happy now because that's never happening again."

His smile turned deadly. He pushed off the desk.

"You can deny it all you want, but I heard you. I know what you really want. There's no going back now."

He stepped around her. She thought he was going to leave, but instead, he shoved her against the desk. He pressed himself against her, his front flush with her back. One hand wrapped around her neck, the other curled over her waist. His breath hot against her ear.

"You think you're going to win this, don't you?"

She couldn't answer him. Fear, anger and desire clashed inside her.

"You feel that. You feel what you do to me every time I look at you."

He ground himself against her behind. It left no room for doubt.

"Yes," she whimpered.

"Are you sure you don't want me to fuck you right now?"

"Yes."

"I don't believe a word that's coming out of your mouth. You see, I can feel how much you want me. How much you crave me. How much you need me to bend you over and fuck you on my desk until you're begging me for a release."

Holy fucking hell. Why is he doing this to me?

He ground into her again. She whimpered. She was so wet, it was practically running down her thighs.

"Say yes, Candace. Say yes for me."

"No."

"Wrong answer."

He hadn't even trapped her arms, but she felt frozen on the spot. He'd shattered her resolve. Broken her will. All she wanted was for him to do exactly what he pleased with her. His fingers trailed down her stomach.

"Don't," she whispered.

He ignored her, flipping open the button of her jeans. The zip came next, but he didn't move to try to take them off her. His fingers brushed over her. She trembled, jolts running up her spine. She knew what was coming next, but she couldn't bring herself to stop him. His fingers dipped below her underwear. He growled when he felt her.

"Is this what I do to you?" he whispered hoarsely.

His fingers circled her core. She shuddered, whimpering.

"Answer me."

"You fucking know the answer," she replied.

"I want to hear you say it."

She didn't want to admit anything to him at all. Every time she gave him an inch, he took a mile.

"Yes, for fuck's sake, yes. Every single fucking time you're near me. Damn you. I fucking hate you and yet you're consuming me with every damn breath I take. Why are you doing this to me? Why can't you just leave me be?"

"I want you."

He says it like it's that fucking simple.

"And I know you want me."

His fingers became more insistent. Everything was on fire. She was done trying to resist him at that moment. He pressed hot kisses to her neck, just below her ear. The heat between them was too much. She ground against him. He hissed, pressing her closer. She could feel him pulsating against her rear. It only heightened her need.

"Please," she whispered.

"What are you asking for?"

"I can't take it, please."

"Do you want to come all over my fingers?"

"Yes," she whimpered, utterly unable to lie to him.

"All you had to do was ask."

His fingers increased their pace. She moved against him, needing so much to end this sinfully delicious torture at his hands.

"Fuck, don't stop," he grunted.

She ground against him harder. She could feel him everywhere. It was as though his hands were running across every part of her body. So close. She was so close. His breath was hot and heavy. She panted.

I can't take it. I need him. I need him. How can I ever turn back now?

The tightly wound cord inside her snapped. Her eyes rolled back in her head and she could've sworn she saw stars in her vision. It rushed through her at an alarming pace. The intense pleasure was unlike anything else. Crying out as her legs began to buckle underneath her. Her hands slammed down on the desk, but he kept her anchored to him. She trembled and bucked against him.

"Fuck," he growled.

She felt him shuddering against her back and she knew he'd come right along with her.

Shit. Shit. Fuck. Holy fucking hell.

His hand fell away from her neck, dropping down on the table beside hers. He removed his other hand, placing it on the desk. She was still caught between him and it. They were both out of breath. Nothing could have ever prepared her for that and they hadn't even fucked each other.

"I think I want to argue with you again," he said.

"Why the hell would you want that?"

"Because it turned you on and you couldn't deny me any longer."

She shut her mouth, absolutely hating that he was right. Fighting with him had turned her on to the point where she thought she was going to combust on the spot. And his brutal kiss had only made it worse.

"Are you happy now you've broken through my resolve?" she asked.

"No. That wasn't enough. It'll never be enough until I've had all of you. Perhaps not even then."

His forefinger on his left hand curled over her pinkie finger. The gesture was almost her complete undoing. She turned her face towards where his was resting on her shoulder. His dark eyes glittered in the light.

"Lucifer…"

"Yes?"

"Is this just about breaking me or is there more to it?"

"Who said anything about breaking?"

"Answer the question."

He grinned, running the tip of his tongue over his bottom lip. It made her want to kiss him. She shifted, turning around in his embrace. She was still stuck between him and the desk. He stared down at her, eyes questioning.

She reached up, curling her hand around the back of his neck before pulling him towards her. The kiss was soft, tentative and almost gentle. It was a far cry from the brutal way they'd kissed each other before. One hand curled around her back, the other was in her hair, cradling her face.

How can he be so tender now after what happened between us?

It made her heart ache. She hadn't expected Lucifer to be gentle at all. He pulled away, resting his forehead against hers.

"Do you think me incapable of treating you with care?"

"You heard that?"

"Hmm, I think kissing you allows me to."

Well, that's just great. How am I going to control my thoughts when he kisses me? Fuck. Why am I even thinking about kissing him again?

It was a mistake. She knew it was, but she couldn't bring herself to deny she wanted him kissing her. She wanted that gentleness and yet she wanted all his brutality too.

"You still haven't answered my question."

"Question?"

"Don't try and play coy with me now. You know what I asked you."

He smiled. It was deadly. His thumb ran over her swollen bottom lip. It was still a little sensitive from when he'd bitten her. She hadn't forgiven him for doing that.

He punished me and fuck, do I want him to continue to do so, again and again.

"I'm not just going to break you," he whispered. "I'm going to ruin you completely."

Chapter Six

The words played over and over in her head.

I'm going to ruin you completely.

They'd been on a loop for days. It wasn't like time passed here in the same way, but she still tried to count the number of days she'd been in Hell. Two and a half weeks almost.

Despite their strained relationship, she was sure her father would be concerned she'd disappeared without a trace. Would Jax have told him? Surely her best friend wouldn't keep her father in the dark. She didn't really know whether or not Jax had known he'd sent her to Hell. She didn't want to doubt her best friend, but something had been off that night.

When he'd created the portal, he'd grabbed hold of her, his eyes wild with fear, concern. He was almost frantic.

"Go, Cadmi. Go. You know as well as I do what will happen if you don't leave."

He'd thrown her head first without giving her a chance to respond. And she'd ended up here, on top of the man who haunted her every waking moment.

And everything seems to always come back to him. Damn it.

He hadn't come near her since that day, yet again keeping his distance. He was toying with her. She knew it. And she was falling headlong into his trap regardless.

Cursing herself, she rolled out of bed and got dressed. She was going to do something productive today. She'd managed to convince Mall to allow her to help with their research into how to get around Hell's new rules. She grabbed breakfast before following the directions the succubus had given her.

"Down the hall, through the last door on the right," she muttered to herself.

Knowing she would be in for a heck of a talking to if she took a wrong turn, she carefully turned the handle on the door. Mall sat behind a desk, tapping away on a laptop. The room was decorated in varying shades of purple. She looked up when Candace stepped in.

"Did you sleep well?" she asked.

"Um, yes, thanks," Candace replied.

Mall stood, coming around her desk. She pointed to the other desk in the room.

"You can work with me here. Perhaps a fresh set of eyes will help."

Candace sat down at the desk she indicated. Mall walked over and leant towards her, pointing at the laptop.

"I've provided you with my notes. You'll see I have marked several books as being relevant, but I have not yet had a chance to ask my Lord for them. They are in his private collection."

"You mean in his bedroom?"

"Yes, which you have access to."

Candace almost choked. It brought back memories of what Lucifer had done to her only days ago against his desk.

I'm going to ruin you completely.

Her face felt like it was on fire.

"So, um, you want me to go through them?"

"After you've made yourself familiar with where we are, yes. This is not an easy task. We have been working for quite a while and yet we are still no further forward."

"I see."

"Please let me know if you have questions."

Mall turned away and went back to her desk. Candace stared at the screen for a moment.

I'm going to ruin you completely.

She had to damn well stop thinking about that. Had to stop thinking about how much she wanted to march into his throne room, get down on her knees and beg him. Beg him to end her suffering. The suffering he'd brought on after that damn day he'd kissed her. After their explosive argument had boiled over. After he'd touched her in ways she'd swore she'd never let him.

And still it wasn't enough.

She wanted more.

She wanted everything.

She shook herself. Thinking about him was a bad idea. She settled down to read over Mall's notes. They had a lot of ideas, but too many dead ends.

After a couple of hours, her head hurt, and she felt like her mind was about to explode. She sat back, kneading her eyes with her palms.

"It's a lot to take in."

She jumped at the sound of Mall's voice.

"Um, yes... There's a lot of things I don't really understand. I guess you want me for my knowledge of magic rather than the more technical stuff?"

"Yes, a solution using magic could work if we knew the right way to go about it."

Candace nodded slowly, slumping in the chair. She couldn't really think of a solution at that moment. She was incapable of creating portals, but she understood how the process worked. Perhaps similar principals could be applied to the situation with Hell. If you could use a portal to get in, then getting out should be simple. Right?

"Perhaps you should take a break. See if you can find those books for me? I put the list on that tablet next to you," Mall said.

Candace stood up, stretching before giving Mall a nod. She picked up the tablet next to the laptop and strode out of the room. She made a beeline straight for Lucifer's bedroom. It was empty. A stab of disappointment ran through her, but she shook it off.

What else did I expect? He's busy.

She looked down at the list on the tablet. There were at least twenty titles. She wondered how Lucifer had categorised the ones on his bookshelves. She placed the tablet on the desk, memorising the first one on the list before starting on the far side, looking over each of the spines.

"Why am I not surprised Mall asked you to go through my library?"

She jumped, stumbling backwards into his chest. His hands gripped her arms, steadying her. She craned her head back, staring up at Lucifer with

43

wide eyes. She'd been completely distracted by all the books, she hadn't even realised he'd come in.

"You scared me."

"Anything to get you in my arms."

She scowled, turning around and facing him properly.

"Funny that. You're the one who's stayed away from me since..."

She couldn't finish the sentence. Her face grew hot.

I'm going to ruin you completely.

He looked her up and down, eyes darkening. A sly smile appeared on his lips. He damn well knew exactly what she was referring to.

"Did you want me near you?"

"I... That... You... That's not the point."

"No? Should we not talk about how much you enjoyed it when I had you up against my desk?"

She spluttered, taking a step back. No. She didn't want to talk about it. She didn't want to remember how it had felt to have his hands on her.

"Lost for words? Well, perhaps now isn't the time for talking anyway."

He gave her no warning, slamming her against the bookcase before his mouth connected with hers. Her hands were pinned above her head with one of his. Everything was on fire in an instant.

"Are you ready to give in?"

No. I already told you. I'm never giving into you.

He pulled away, eyes glittering with amusement. She wanted to be defiant. To tell him to leave her alone, but the other half of her wanted him to have his way. His free hand cupped her face, his thumb running over her bottom lip.

"You're only delaying the inevitable. I will break you."

I will ruin you completely.

Why was it so hot? Why did she want him to ruin her? The worst part of it all. She was so close to letting him.

"Just kiss me," she whispered.

His eyebrow arched up, a smirk appearing on his face. He leant back towards her. His mouth was so close, yet so far.

"Aren't you going to ask me nicely?"

Why does he have to make this into a battle between us? I can't take it. I need him to give me everything I crave.

"Please."

He uttered a low growl. His mouth was on hers the next instant. It wasn't gentle nor sweet. His kiss was demanding and she relented, completely. He let go of her hands, his fingers tangling in her hair. She gripped his shoulders, nails digging into his shirt. She wanted it all and more.

"Where would you like it this time? Against the desk again or perhaps you'd like me to take you to bed?"

Get out of my head.

The heat between them was unbearable. She couldn't think straight. Lucifer had taken command of everything. She dropped one of her arms, holding onto his waist, feeling the hard muscle between her fingertips.

This wasn't anger filled lust this time. It was the fervour brought on by pent up frustration bubbling over. He was right. It wasn't enough. It would never be enough until they'd taken everything from each other. He was going to possess her in ways no other man ever could.

He grabbed her hand and shoved it in between them, forcing her to touch him. She groaned into his mouth. She wanted to touch him there and everywhere. He'd broken her resolve yet again. This man was the Devil through and through, but it only made her crave him all the more.

"I am not a patient man," he growled, releasing her mouth.

"My answer is the same. No," she replied, out of breath.

He pulled away, placing his hands on her shoulders and shoving her to her knees. He held onto her hair at the back of her head. His grip was so tight it made her wince.

"Every time you deny me, I will punish you. Is this what you want?"

She reached up, trying to tug his hand away.

"No," she whimpered.

"Oh, I think you do. You want me to show you no mercy. I told you. I'm going to ruin you. You'll never be free of me. Do you understand? Never."

His other hand went to his belt buckle and in one swift move he had it undone. She barely had time to formulate any sort of response. Her eyes widened to saucers when he revealed exactly what he was packing. She'd felt his cock under her hand but feeling and seeing were two very different things.

"This time, you're going to pleasure me."

She put a hand out to try and stop him, but it was too late. He tugged her towards him by her hair. She had little time to take a breath before he was half in her mouth. She tried not to gag.

What the fuck?

Putting both her hands on his thighs, she tried to push back. He held her hair tighter, forcing her into taking more.

I can't breathe. God, he's huge. But it feels so fucking hot. I'm clearly fucked up in the head for finding this a turn on.

Her arousal was practically running down her legs. He began to move her head back and forth, building a steady rhythm. He grunted, his other hand slammed on the bookcase.

"Fuck. Being inside your mouth is sweet, delicious torture."

He pumped his cock in and out of her mouth with a forcefulness that made her jaw ache. There was nothing she could do but give into him. She wasn't quite sure when it changed from him forcing her to her wrapping her hand around the base of him and taking over. His fingers dug into her skull.

"Fuck, Candace. Fuck."

Their pace increased. She wanted to give him pleasure. She wanted him to fall down the rabbit hole with her.

"Touch yourself."

She complied, so turned on, it wouldn't take much for her to reach a conclusion with him. The edge of the cliff was rapidly approaching, and it was all she could do to hold on for dear life. The moment they both hurtled off it exploded like wildfire. He grunted, pulsating in her mouth as she trembled, barely able to hold herself up.

His hand fell away from her hair. He panted, dark eyes wild and unfocused. She released him, falling onto her hands and taking deep gulps of air, trying to force it into her lungs. Still shaking uncontrollably.

"Fuck you," she whispered.

"I think you'll find you just fucked me. I knew you were going to be exquisite, but this was something else."

He knelt beside her, taking her face in his hand. His touch was gentle. She felt something wash over her and with immediacy, her jaw stopped aching.

"I'm not sorry I hurt you," he whispered.

"I hate you."

He leant closer, kissing her with tenderness. She shifted off her hands, grabbing hold of him and pulling him closer. Completely unable to help herself.

I want him even though he is fucking with my head. Damn it.

"You can't hide your true feelings from me. I'm going to have all of you. You and I both know it."

He was right.

And she hated him for it.

Chapter Seven

Candace couldn't sleep. Tossing and turning in the bed until she felt like her head would explode. Utterly consumed by what happened between her and Lucifer earlier. He'd left the room not long after he'd kissed her so thoroughly she almost told him to take her to bed and finish what they'd started. She could still taste him on her tongue. It was torture. All of it. He was drowning her. She was never going to be able to come up for air whilst she was still stuck down here with him.

There was only one thing for it. She had to get out of here before he completely destroyed her. Before all her secrets were spilled. That couldn't happen. She could never give into him. She had no choice but to find a way to leave Hell.

It all came back to Jax and why he'd done this in the first place. She was sure he knew where he was sending her. But why? Why would he do this? And how? It took a shit ton of power to open a portal between Hell and Earth. Jax didn't have enough juice as far as she was aware.

He couldn't possibly have done this because of what was going to happen when she turned twenty-five. The thought made her pause. It was only a few months away now. She'd resigned herself to the fact it was happening. There was no other choice. She'd been given time to lead her life as she pleased. Everything was going to change.

Had Jax really sent her down here to save her from her own miserable fate? She shook herself. It couldn't be that. She'd never once complained about it to him. No, Jax wouldn't do something that reckless or stupid. There had to be another reason.

I just have to be patient and ask him when I return to Earth.

She wasn't going to be able to sleep anytime soon. She sat up, turning on the lamp and picking up one of the books Mall had asked her to go through. It was better to do something useful then sit around driving herself crazy. It was a spell book. She hated reading these as they were always so complex and usually in Latin.

Sighing, she opened the first page and settled in. *I was right. This is in Latin.* Her father had made sure she learnt it from a young age, but she hated it all the same.

After only half an hour, her head hurt. This was a nightmare. None of the spells in this book were helpful. There was nothing to do with portal magic. She was sure that would be the best way of getting out of here. There had to be some way to bend the rules.

Flipping through the book, she landed on something she'd never seen before.

Et inferorum regnum. The Kingdom of Hell.

It was an entire section devoted to the place. She scanned through it. There was a lot of stuff she didn't really understand, but one thing stuck out to her. *Porta ad infernum.* It spoke of how to open a gateway to Hell. It was a complex spell. She wondered if she could reverse this and create a gateway to Earth.

There was only one thing for it. She had to show this to Mall.

Slipping a bookmark into the relevant page, she closed the book and leapt out of bed. She was wearing sleep shorts and a t-shirt, but she couldn't be bothered to change. It wouldn't matter. She'd show this to Mall and come straight back to bed. Hopefully she could sleep after this.

Keeping the book close to her chest, she slipped into the hallway. When she got to Mall's door, she knocked twice. There was no answer. She tried the handle and it opened. There was no one in the room. She sighed. That was a bust. Perhaps Mall was busy.

Closing the door, she was about to go back to the bedroom when she heard the faint sound of voices. She looked towards the double doors at the end of the hall. One of them was slightly ajar. Lucifer told her she wasn't permitted in his throne room.

Curiosity got the better of her. She tiptoed over to the opening, looking through the crack. She could just about make out a huge, hulking demon with large horns. She stifled a gasp.

"With all due respect, my Lord, this matter has gone on for long enough. Your reassurances are meaningless without proof you are doing something about it," the demon said.

"As our Lord has told you on several occasions. This is not a simple task." That was Mall's voice.

So that's where she is. I guess I should come back later.

She was about to turn and leave when the demon turned his head. His black eyes met hers. Her pulse spiked, fear running through her. She backed away, but the demon stormed over to the door, pushed it open and grabbed her by the arm. He tugged her into the room and threw her down at the steps that led up to the dais where Lucifer's throne sat. The book tumbled out of her hands, clattering on the floor loudly. Her knees hurt from the impact with the floor.

She looked up slowly. When her eyes met Lucifer's, she knew she was in the shit. He looked oddly calm, his expression almost bored. He was leaning on his fingers, the other hand drumming on the arm of his throne. He looked every bit the King of Hell dressed in a neat black suit. She knew underneath that façade he was angry.

"What is this human doing in your private rooms?" the demon asked.

"Is that really any of your business, Beleth?" Lucifer replied, his tone neutral.

Candace was frozen on the floor, unable to look away from him. She didn't want to say anything to make this situation worse.

"It is when we have spent months being unable to leave and suddenly, a girl turns up."

"She is none of your concern."

"No? Then you won't mind me taking her."

The demon grab her hair and haul her up off the floor. She struggled against his grip, but he wrapped a hand around her neck.

"A pretty little thing, aren't you?" he said in her ear.

She froze, staring at Lucifer with wide eyes.

Was he going to do anything to stop this?

Beleth was sorely trying Lucifer's patience. He was touching Candace. His hand was on her throat. It enraged him, tension rippling through his body, but he kept a lid on it.

"Release her," he said.

"Why? She is a worthless human," Beleth replied, his smile gleeful.

"Because she is mine. You are well aware I do not share my toys with anyone."

Candace's eyes flashed with anger. He didn't acknowledge it. Beleth looked at the girl.

"This little thing? I thought you had more refined tastes, my Lord."

Lucifer's hand curled around the arm of his throne. The only outward expression of his anger. Candace was not a little thing. She was beautiful, alluring and he could barely keep his hands off her. Beleth didn't need to know any of those things.

"I will not say it again. Release her."

Beleth ran his other hand down her front. Lucifer was going to rip his hand from his wrist in a moment. Candace was his and his alone. He didn't care what she said. He owned her body and having Beleth put his grubby paws on her drove him crazy.

"I suppose she might have her assets. I could sure use a distraction."

"Beleth, take your hand off her. Now."

Something caught his eye. Pink smoke swirled in Candace's hand. It moved up her arm, turning it blue in the process as it curled up around her shoulder and underneath Beleth's hand on her throat. A moment later, Beleth roared and threw her away from him, clutching his hand to his chest. She fell to the floor, scrambling away towards the stairs.

When she looked up at Lucifer, her face was a picture of fear and anger.

"Come here," he said.

She got to her feet and walked up the steps. When she reached him, he grabbed her arm and tugged her into his lap. She yelped, turning around to glare at him. He turned her face back towards the demon.

"If you know what's good for you, you'll play along," he whispered in her ear.

He could feel her trembling, but she folded her hands in her lap. She was being compliant.

Good girl.

He indicated to Mall that she should pick up the book which was on the floor. The succubus strolled over, leaning down to snatch it up before Beleth's attention fell on it. There had to be a reason Candace had that book on her.

"That fucking bitch has magic," Beleth said, his expression sullen.

"I did tell you to let her go," Lucifer replied.

"Are you just going to let her get away with that?"

Lucifer rolled his eyes, curling a hand around Candace's jaw and turning it to the side so he could access her neck.

"Rest assured, Beleth. I will punish her."

He ran his tongue down the side of her throat, eyes on the demon. Beleth was fuming. He could see the anger in his duke's eyes. Lucifer's other hand was on her thigh, travelling upwards. Candace's breath came a little faster, but she remained silent.

"Your assurances mean nothing to me."

"No?"

He nudged her hands out of the way as he continued his path upwards. When his fingers brushed over her core, she shifted in his lap. It made him harden instantly. She stiffened. His hand tightened on her jaw, sending her a message. She had to play along. Beleth was eying Lucifer's wandering hands with a raised eyebrow.

"No. What is she and why is she here?"

"Well, as you've gathered, she possesses magic. You do the math. She's my toy, Beleth. Mine. Aren't you?"

His mouth was close to her ear. He was touching her in earnest now through her clothes. She wriggled in his lap. It was not helping matters. He ached to bury himself in her. Being inside her mouth earlier was the sweetest ecstasy.

Despite her protests that she hated him, she'd enjoyed every second of their encounter. He'd heard it loud and clear in her head afterwards. She wanted him.

"Yes, my Lord," she replied. "I am yours."

Those words were almost his undoing. He kissed her neck again, trying to keep a lid on his burning need.

Everything about her is driving me to distraction. I need to fuck this girl until she cannot take any more. We both need each other. I know it. She knows it.

"You see? She is very compliant. Apologise to Beleth for me and this matter will be settled."

"I am very sorry."

Beleth's eyes narrowed.

"Now, if you don't mind, I wish to be alone with my toy."

"This isn't over, my Lord. There is still the matter of the gates being sealed."

His eyes snapped to the demon. This conversation was most definitely over. Beleth needed to learn his place.

"Mall, escort him from the room before I decide he needs a turn in the pit."

Mall sauntered over to Beleth. He glared at the both of them but turned on his heel and stormed out.

There was silence for a long moment. Candace tore herself out of his lap. Her face was bright red, her breath coming fast. Her eyes were wild with fury. She slapped him across the cheek, the noise ringing through the room.

"Go fuck yourself," she hissed before stomping away towards the door and slamming it behind her.

Lucifer sighed, resting his chin on his hand. Mall raised an eyebrow at him. He shook his head. Her reaction was not unexpected.

"I suppose I better go deal with that," he said, getting to his feet.

"You know, if you want to get on her good side, you might want to be a little more considerate and not subject her to such things," Mall said. "That was a little overboard, don't you think?"

"Did I ask your opinion?"

She rolled her eyes, hoisting the book up on her chest.

"I might be a demon, my Lord, but I also understand women. She is stuck down here against her will and doesn't want to admit how much it affects her. If you want her to come to you willingly, you might want to keep that in mind."

He pointed to the book.

"She had that on her for a reason. Find out what it is."

He walked down the steps towards the double doors which led to his private chambers. He turned back to Mall.

"How do you know I want her to come to me willingly?"

"It doesn't take a genius. I've seen the way you two look at each other. Be gentle with her. I suspect she's a little more fragile than she lets on."

He frowned. Candace wasn't fragile. She was fiery and wild. Mall wouldn't say such a thing to him without reason.

He turned on his heel and walked out of the room, preparing himself for the fallout from the incident with Beleth.

Chapter Eight

When he reached the living room, she was pacing back and forth, clear agitation on her face. He shut the door behind him, taking a few steps towards her. Mall's words rang in his ears.

Be gentle with her.

He may have crossed a line by touching her up in front of Beleth, but he was trying to make a point. She was his and his demons needed to be put in their place. He just didn't know what to say to her now. He wasn't sure anything he did say would appease her.

She stopped in the middle of the room, turning to him. Her violet eyes blazed, but it wasn't rage in her expression. She strode towards him and then her mouth was on his. She pushed him until his back hit the door, still kissing him furiously. A little confused by her sudden change of mood, he kissed her back, his fingers curling in her hair.

Candace?

He knew she'd heard him, but she didn't respond. She grabbed one of his hands, pulling it down in between them and under her clothes. His fingers met her softness. She was so hot and wet, it coated them in an instant. She let go of his hand, curling it around his back.

"Finish what you started."

It was the last thing he expected from her. Part of him wanted to deny her, but her heat drove him crazy. He wanted to feel her. Pressing his fingers inside her, his thumb on her core, he felt her shudder against him. She groaned into his mouth, pressing closer. She was like a furnace.

"Please, I don't want to beg you. You're a fucking arsehole for subjecting me to that shit."

And yet you want me anyway.

"Lucifer, I swear if you don't make me come, I'm going to fucking explode."

He worked his fingers inside her. She released his mouth, breathing hard as she pressed her face into his shoulder.

"Damn you," she whispered. "I can't do this anymore. It's not fair. All I want is to give into you and I can't."

He wrapped his other arm around her, pressing her closer. What could he say to that? If he insisted she tell him why, she'd quite possibly storm off in the middle of him pleasuring her. She turned her face up to look at him. Her violet eyes were full of desire tapered with turmoil.

"Lucifer..."

"You just demanded I make you come. Do you want to talk or should I continue?"

She was silent for several moments. He stilled, wondering exactly what was going through her head. She seemed very conflicted.

"I don't want to talk."

He cocked an eyebrow.

"Then what do you want?"

She bit her lip.

"You."

"Excuse me, did I just hear you correctly?"

She looked down at his chest, her face going an interesting shade of red.

"Just take me to bed."

He pulled his hand from her shorts before hoisting her up. She wrapped her legs around his waist as he strode towards the bedroom.

"This doesn't mean I'm going to let you fuck me," she said, staring down at him.

"We'll see about that."

He tossed her on the bed, crawling over her in an instant. Her fingers curled into his suit jacket, pushing it off his shoulders. His mouth was on hers. He needed to feel her heat again, but this time he wanted to bury himself in her. Nothing was going to get in the way.

I want to see the real you, Candace.

58

"What?"

You heard me.

She turned her face from his, breaking the contact between them.

"I already told you no."

"You're mine whether you are on board with it or not."

She turned back to him, her expression thunderous.

"Oh, so on top of being an arsehole, you're a possessive jerk too. This was a stupid idea."

She pushed at his chest. He smiled. There was the fire he'd come to expect from her.

"Oh, no, you don't get to stop now."

He shoved aside her shorts and underwear, burying his fingers in her heat. She arched up against him, fingers digging into his shirt.

"Fuck," she groaned.

"Mmm, that's it. I want to hear you moan."

Brushing his thumb over her core, she stared up at him with wide eyes, shuddering. This was exactly what he wanted to see. Her at his mercy. He leant down, kissing her neck and up her jaw. One of her hands curled into his hair, the other gripping the sheets. A moan escaped her mouth when his fingers became more insistent.

"This is what you asked for. Don't forget that. You said it, Candace, you want me. You want me all over you. Touching every inch of your skin. Nothing between us whilst I fuck you until you can't walk for days."

She moaned again, her eyes fluttering closed.

"Tell me that's not exactly what you want."

She shook her head, arching against him. Her fingers dug into his head.

"Say it."

"Lucifer..."

"Say. It."

"Yes," she whispered. "Yes, I want you to do all those things."

"Are you going to let me?"

"No. You know that."

He growled, biting down on her neck. She cried out, shuddering. She was close. He could feel it pulsating in her veins. He was so hard, straining against his trousers. She was the most frustrating woman he'd ever met. If he didn't have her soon, he'd lose it completely.

She'll be the death of me. I'm going to make her mine. My little witch.

He didn't know why he needed her submission. He could take what he wanted. Candace wouldn't forgive him for it. That seemed to matter to him.

He growled again, pressing his fingers deeper inside her. She was so slick and hot. It drove him insane. Her fingers dug harder into his hair. He felt it the moment she snapped. She clenched around his fingers, trembling as she cried out.

"Lucifer!"

His name on her lips made him ache further. Frustration tore at him. How long was she going to make him wait?

When she opened her eyes again, he was leaning over her using both hands to prop himself up.

"Better?" he asked.

"It'll never be better. Not when we're near each other."

"What does that mean?"

"It means unless we fuck, I'm never going to feel better."

That made him smirk.

No, she's right. It won't feel better until then. Whenever then might be.

"The offer still stands."

"I shouldn't admit these things to you."

"No?"

"You'll use it against me, but right now, I don't care. I'm tired of doing the right thing. I'm tired of having so many expectations weighing down on me." She closed her eyes again. "What's the point in caring when I'm stuck here? What if I can never go home?"

A tear slipped down her right cheek. He wasn't sure why the sight of it made him feel like holding her close and never letting go. He brushed it away with his thumb, cupping her cheek.

"I'll find a way to send you home."

Her eyes flew open.

"What?"

"You don't belong here. You should be on Earth. Hell is no place for a living soul."

It didn't matter how much he wanted her. He knew what it meant to be caged. Locked away and forced to do your duty.

"That's not something I expected to hear from you."

"You must know why I was cast down from Heaven. Freedom is a precious commodity."

She reached up, brushing the lock of hair which had fallen in his face away.

"I'm sorry."

"What are you apologising for?"

"Here I am complaining when I've barely been away for a month and yet you've not been able to go home for millennia."

"Don't tell me you feel sorry for me?"

She frowned.

"Having empathy is not the same as feeling sorry for someone. You know, I thought for one moment you might want to have a proper conversation with me."

For some reason, it bothered him that she felt something for him other than lust, anger or desire. She wasn't meant to have feelings for the Devil. He didn't deserve that.

"I still meant what I said. I'll help you go home."

"After you have your way with me."

"Candace, contrary to what you might think, I am not a mindless animal driven by lust for you."

She raised an eyebrow.

Clearly, she has no idea how much I've had to hold back when it comes to her. I want to give her pleasure, pain and everything in between. I want her splayed out before me, unable to do anything but give into me.

"Then why do all our conversations escalate into something sexual?"

"It takes two to tango. Don't put it all on me."

"You are so frustrating. If you really want to know why I keep saying no, perhaps try to get to know me."

She shoved at his chest. He took her hands, pinning them to the bed. She glared at him. Getting to know her would mean seeing her as something other than the woman he wanted to ruin. That would cross a line he wasn't sure he could come back from.

61

"We are not finished talking. Why were you near my throne room in the first place?"

She sighed, looking away.

"I found something in that book and I wanted to tell Mall about it."

"What did you find?"

"A spell. It opens a gateway to Hell, but I think I can reverse it if I have the right things."

"And open a gateway to Earth?"

She nodded, turning back to him. If she could do that, it would solve all of his problems with Hell and his dukes would leave him alone.

"Are you skilled enough to do such a thing?"

"I don't know. My magic is an anomaly because of my fae blood. My father never tried to fully test my capabilities."

"Then I will go over it with Mall."

He needed to get to the bottom of it with his assistant. He let go of her wrists to move off her, but she grabbed his arm. He looked down at her with a frown.

"Don't go."

"What?"

"I don't want you to go."

Her violet eyes were cautious.

She doesn't want me to leave? What is this now?

"I couldn't sleep, that's why I was reading that book. I don't want to be alone."

"I am not here to make you feel at ease."

"I... that's not what I meant. Why is this so difficult to say?" She blinked. "I'd like it if you stayed with me because I want you here, not because I'm lonely."

He was momentarily at a loss for words. Something about the girl below him disarmed him. He didn't want to feel things. Especially not for a woman who drove him crazy with lust.

Be gentle with her.

Mall's words rang in his ears again. He sighed, shifting off her and lying down on his side. He clicked his fingers and was instantly in less restrictive clothing. A plain t-shirt and loose bottoms.

She eyed him for a moment as if she was waiting for him to change his mind. She shifted closer, burying her face in his chest, her arm around his waist. He stared down at her, utterly confused by the girl wrapped around him.

He reached out, tugging the covers over the both of them before curling his free arm around her. He'd never lain in bed with a woman like this before. It had always been about sex and he usually left right after.

She's cuddling me. This feels... wrong and yet right at the same time.

He fought against the urge to bury his face in her hair.

"You're warm," she mumbled.

"Am I allowed to ask why you're... holding me?"

"I like having you close. Why? Do you not make a habit of this?"

"No. Never."

She turned her face up, staring at him with wide eyes.

"Are you saying I'm the first person you've let cuddle you?"

He didn't want to answer her at all, but the way she was looking at him made his heart thump.

"Yes."

A small smile appeared on her lips before she buried her face back in his chest.

"So, the Devil has a soft spot for me," she whispered.

"I do not."

"Yes, you do, Lucifer. I've admitted so much to you. It's only fair you be honest with me."

Disarming. Candace was utterly disarming. He couldn't deny he felt more than just desire for the woman pressed against him.

"If I admit to such a thing, you're to keep it to yourself. Do you understand?"

"Yes. You have a reputation to uphold."

He buried his face in her hair, breathing her in. She smelt of citrus and violets, like her beautiful eyes which enraptured him.

"I will treat you with care when you ask for it," he whispered. "And I will punish you when you disobey me. I won't be gentle then. You'll feel the full force of my brutality. Are we clear?"

"Yes. Very."

Her hand brushed over his side, falling in between them. Her fingers ran over his stomach and lower until she'd wrapped her hand around him. He stiffened, pulling away from her slightly.

"What are you doing?"

"Let me touch you," she replied, staring up at him with such tenderness it made his heart hammer in his chest.

What is this? Why does she make me feel this way?

He didn't stop her when she released his cock from the confines of his clothes. Her small hand stroked up and down the length of him at a slow pace. Even that simple touch sent his body into overdrive. Nerve endings tingling with anticipation.

"Candace," he hissed.

"Shh, let me take care of you."

She pressed her mouth to his, kissing him softly. His fingers curled into her t-shirt, gripping it as she moved faster. After making her come earlier, he was so close to exploding. All the pent-up lust he felt slammed into him with a force which made him shiver. This woman had no idea what she did to him.

"I want to give into you, but there are things you don't know about me. Things I can never change."

Then tell me.

"I can't. If I let you have me, I can't walk away from you. You were right. You'll ruin me."

You're already mine. Don't you see that?

She was silent, pulling away from him. Her eyes were sad. She didn't stop touching him and it wasn't long before he shuddered against her, grunting. Even the release didn't put a dampener on his need to have her, but it gave him a moment's relief. She readjusted his clothing before curling her arm back around him and pressing her face to his chest.

"I am yours," she whispered. "And that's what scares me the most."

Chapter Nine

Candace stared at the pentagram within the circle she'd drawn, inspecting each line closely. She'd lost count of the amount of times she'd attempted to get this right. Mall had given her a large empty room to work in. Various herbs, plants and candles were scattered about the place. It wasn't easy to reverse engineer a spell when you had no idea what you were doing. She wished she'd paid more attention in her father's lessons.

"This should be right," she muttered to herself.

Getting up, she picked up the necessary candles, placing one at each end of the pentagram. Next, she dumped the relevant items into the bowl near her feet. This was an experiment. She'd adjusted the amounts yet again. She understood the basics, but there was so much about spellcraft which eluded her.

She'd ended up with several more books to try to work out the right way to go about this. It'd taken a full week of research before she felt ready to put the spell to the test.

The door opened behind her.

"Dare I ask how it's going?" Mall said.

"Probably wise not to," Candace replied.

Mall arrived next to her, staring down at the pentagram. She hadn't asked too many questions about what Candace was doing, only providing her with the necessary ingredients. Candace didn't much care where Mall had got this stuff from.

"Looks complicated."

"It is, and it isn't. The basic construction never varies, but there are changes depending on the function. This was the one thing I was always good at. It's the rest I struggle with. The books help to an extent, but as you know, this isn't as simple as following a recipe."

"How long have you been at this?"

Candace looked down at her watch. It was the only way she was still able to keep track of how long she'd been here.

"Um, five hours or so."

"My Lord would not be pleased you're neglecting yourself."

Candace scowled. A reminder of Lucifer wasn't what she needed right now. The memory of the night they'd shared together made her shiver. It was the first time they'd had a serious conversation with each other that hadn't ended up in an argument.

She'd fallen asleep tucked up in his arms and he'd still been there when she woke up. A slow languid kiss had followed whilst his fingers roamed under her t-shirt, down her back. She could still feel the phantom touch even though it had been two weeks. He'd left and given her breakfast in bed. He'd not even attempted to get her to give into him. And the way he'd smiled made her heart thump uncomfortably in her chest. She didn't want feelings for Lucifer, but there they were anyway. Haunting her.

"I'll go hassle him for a meal after this."

Mall grinned at her. Candace had found a sort of kinship with the succubus. Mall wasn't afraid to talk back to Lucifer nor did she take any shit from anyone. It seemed the Devil didn't mind the succubus giving him a hard time because she was good at her job.

"It is strange the way he behaves when you're around."

Candace frowned. She wasn't aware he behaved any differently towards her, except perhaps he was a little more unforgiving towards his subjects. She hadn't seen any other demons since she'd accidentally wound up in the throne room. It was something she could only be glad of. Meeting Beleth hadn't been a pleasant experience.

"What do you mean?"

"I have never seen him have consideration for anyone other than himself, but he always makes sure you are taken care of. Between you and me, you're good for him."

Candace was silent, unable to form a suitable response.

She thinks I'm good for him? How can I be? I drive him crazy.

Mall was right about one thing. He did take care of her no matter how busy he was. She wanted to sigh. She was only meant to be in his life for a fleeting moment and yet the more time she spent down here, the less she wanted to return home. The problem was she had responsibilities back on Earth. Ones she couldn't run away from.

"I don't know about that, but I better get on with this before he comes in here and drags me out by my hair."

She smiled at Mall. Staying here with the Devil was not something she could afford to want.

She picked up the tablet from the floor before lighting each candle with a click of her fingers in the right order. She was still trying to get the words right, which didn't help matters. She'd been testing them, so the results were never guaranteed.

"You're welcome to watch," she said to Mall. "I'm not sure what will happen this time."

Mall took a step back, her expression wary. Candace couldn't blame her. There was no telling what would happen if she got this wrong.

She spoke the first few lines before tossing the last plant in the bowl. It crackled, the bowl lighting up with flame. Continuing the words, she noticed black smoke curling around the bottom of the candles. That hadn't happened before. It concerned her a little.

She uttered the last word. A huge plume of black smoke shot upwards through the ceiling. Candace took several steps back, grabbing Mall and shoving her towards the door.

"Is that supposed to happen?" Mall asked.

"No, definitely not."

The smoke swirled around in the circle like a tornado. When it finally cleared, a man was standing in the centre of it. A man Candace knew very well. His hazel eyes blinked rapidly, his brown hair mussed as if he'd been asleep. He looked down at himself, confusion on his face.

"J... Jax?"

His eyes snapped up to hers, widening in shock.

"Cadmi?"

He took a step towards her, but he bumped into an invisible barrier when he tried to step out of the circle. She remembered she'd put a containment spell around it, just in case something went wrong. This had gone very wrong but not for that reason. How had she managed to bring Jax to Hell?

"What... what have you done?" he asked, looking over the barrier with a frown.

She couldn't speak, the words sticking in her throat. Jax was here. The man who'd sent her to Hell in the first place. She had so many questions.

"Who is this, Candace?" Mall asked.

She turned to the succubus. How would she explain any of this?

"Jaxon. My best friend and the reason I'm here."

And he was stuck here too now because she'd made a mistake with her spell. It hit her. What the hell was Lucifer going to think about this? And how was she going to keep her feelings for Lucifer from Jax?

Fuck. I'm absolutely one hundred percent fucked.

There was nothing she could do about it now.

"Cadmi?" Jax said.

She muttered some words under her breath and the containment field fell. She closed the distance in a few short strides and wrapped her arms around her best friend, bursting into tears immediately.

Jax was the only one she allowed to call her by her middle name. Her fae name her father had told her was chosen by her mother.

He held her close, tucking her head under his chin as he ran a hand down her back.

"Did you bring me to Hell?" he asked.

"You knew you sent me here?"

"Yes."

She pulled away, staring up at him with irritation.

"Why the fuck would you think this was okay, Jax?"

He looked over at where Mall was standing, his hazel eyes narrowing.

"You should know why."

Why was he being so cryptic? Was it because Mall was here? Did he want to speak to her alone?

"But I don't... unless it's because of my birthday."

"Who is that?"

68

"Mallmomoz, Mall. She's... um, well, this is really complicated."

She stepped away from him, wiping her eyes with her sleeve. There were a lot of things she had to explain.

"She's Lucifer's assistant. I've been staying with them and the reason you're here is because we've been trying to work out how to send me back home. No one can leave Hell right now, which you must know because you sent me here."

Jax was silent for several moments before he sighed, running a hand through his hair.

"I'm sorry. I shouldn't have done it, but you understand why, don't you? I know you don't want to go through with all of that even though you never complain about it."

"It was never for you to decide. I've known my whole life. I've accepted it."

Except now she'd met Lucifer. Now she felt things for him that she never wanted to feel. And it made her heart ache knowing she'd have to leave him. She'd told him she'd never be able to walk away from him. To her, leaving and walking away weren't the same thing. Leaving him here when she returned home, that was a given. Walking away from what was between them. Never.

"Can I interject for one moment?" Mall said.

Candace turned to her nodding.

"As much as this is a touching reunion, I have work to attend to and you need to inform my Lord of this new development."

"Right. You're right," Candace replied.

Mall opened the door and indicated that the two of them should follow. Candace grabbed Jax's hand, tugging him along with her.

"Cadmi, who is she talking about?"

"We need to speak to Lucifer."

"What?"

"Lucifer. The Devil. King of Hell. Who else do you think I've been with all this time?"

They left the room and followed Mall down the hallway. Candace wasn't quite sure where Lucifer was.

"I worried about where you'd end up, but the Devil, Cadmi? Have you been okay?"

"I've been fine or as fine as you can be when you're stuck in Hell with no way home because your best friend took it upon himself to save you from your own miserable fate."

She hadn't meant to sound so sullen, but she wasn't exactly best pleased with Jax. Even though it was her fault he was now here.

"Where will he be, Mall?" she asked the succubus who was a few steps ahead of them.

"I will check the throne room for you," Mall replied.

When they reached the door, Mall left them outside. Jax turned to Candace.

"Cadmi, have you really been okay?"

"Yes. I promise. I know you probably won't believe this, but he's fine, mostly."

"Are you really telling me the Devil has been treating you well?"

She didn't want to explain too much about what had really gone on between her and Lucifer, but the truth was, he had been taking care of her.

"Yes, why would I have any reason to lie to you?"

"You wouldn't, but I just... I'm still sorry. I should never have sent you here."

He gripped her shoulders, giving them a squeeze. She put her hand on his chest, sighing. Even though he'd done it for the wrong reasons, she couldn't stay mad at Jax. His hazel eyes were sad. It tore at her heart.

"Honestly, Jax, it's okay."

"Are you sure? This can't have been easy for you."

"I won't deny I'm kind of pissed off with why you did it."

The doors to the throne room slammed open, startling them. She turned her head. Lucifer stood in the doorway. His eyes fell on where her hand was pressed to Jax's chest. His expression turned dark. She immediately dropped her hand, stepping away.

No. No. No. I hope he doesn't think anything of this.

Mall walked out, her eyebrows raised before she strolled down the hallway and went into her office.

Lucifer strode towards her. She knew immediately she was in trouble. Big fucking trouble. He grabbed her arm and tugged her back towards the throne room.

"Cadmi?" Jax called.

She looked back at him, shaking her head.

"Just stay there," she said.

Lucifer dragged her into the throne room, slamming the doors behind them. He pressed her up against one of them, caging her in with his arms.

"What are you doing?" she asked, staring up at him with wide eyes.

"Have you forgotten what you said to me?"

"About what?"

"You are mine, Candace. Mine and only mine."

Chapter Ten

I f she'd known he'd decide to be completely unreasonable when she brought Jax to meet him, she might have run in the other direction.

"I haven't forgotten that, Lucifer. It doesn't mean you get to drag me off for no apparent reason," she replied.

"I don't care who he is. He doesn't get to touch you."

"What the fuck?" She tried to shove him away, but he wouldn't budge. "Jax is my friend and you don't get to dictate shit like that to me. Honestly, are you jealous or something?"

His dark eyes flashed with anger.

"Jealous? I'll show you fucking jealous."

His mouth was on hers, kissing her with ferocity she'd never experienced from him before. His fingers were at her shirt buttons, undoing them one by one, exposing her skin to the air.

When he was done, his hands roamed over her stomach and up to her chest. He cupped one of her breasts, running his thumb over the nub through her bra. It didn't occur to her to push him away. Not when she burnt with longing and need the moment he'd kissed her. Arching up against him, her hands curled around his waist, tugging him closer.

Fuck. I don't want you to stop.

"And yet you're going to tell me to."

She didn't answer him. Her whole body craved his with a desperation that threatened to break her in half. If she didn't have him soon, she would lose her mind. Having never felt this level of need for another person, she was completely out of her depth. No one would ever compare to how he felt against her, his hands on her skin. She wanted Lucifer. She wanted him to ruin her for anyone else. She wanted to be his entirely for now and always. And it was that knowledge which made her turn her face from his.

"I can't do this," she whimpered. "No matter how much I want you."

"You can and you will."

His tongue ran down her neck and lower. Pushing aside her shirt, his dark eyes roamed over her chest. He deftly tugged down her bra on one side, growling when he exposed her breast to the air.

"You are perfect," he whispered. "And all this perfection is mine."

His tongue swept over her nipple, causing her to dig her fingers into his back.

Holy fuck.

"Lucifer... please."

"Only I get to touch you like this."

He bit down. It set all her nerve endings on fire.

"Only you. No one else. You. Always." The words fell out of her mouth against her will. *What the hell am I saying?*

"Say yes and I'll end your torture, Candace. End this torment for both of us."

She wanted to. Every bit of her was screaming out for him. Yet the rational part of her mind told her no.

Not now.

Not ever.

"No."

He tore away from her, running his hand through his hair. There was clear frustration on his face.

"Why do you keep doing this? Explain. Just fucking explain it."

She tugged her shirt closed, suddenly feeling very exposed.

"What if I can't explain it? What if I can't tell you because it fucking kills me that I have absolutely no choice? My life isn't my own, Lucifer. It never has been. Why do you think Jax sent me here? He wanted to save me from my fate."

His hand came up, cupping her face. There was a wild look in his eyes and yet a tenderness in his expression.

"Then let me save you from it."

Tears pricked at the corners of her eyes.

What? He can't. No one can.

"I can't stay here. You know that. You said it yourself. Hell is no place for a living soul."

She reached out, pulling him to her. She curled her arms around his back, pressing her face into his chest. If she could stay like this forever with him, she would do it in a heartbeat.

"When I told you, I can't walk away from you, I meant it, but that doesn't mean I won't have to leave you," she continued. "Because I will. The thought of it makes me want to cry. I didn't want to feel things for you, but I do. It hurts so fucking much. I can't afford to want you. To need you. And yet I do. All I can think about is you. Do you understand why I can't give you what you want? If I do, it'll break me entirely."

He kissed the top of her head before burying his face in her hair.

"Candace..."

"You don't need to say anything. Just stop pushing me. I don't want to go home broken."

She pushed him away, her hands going to her buttons. She quickly adjusted her clothes.

I just lied to him. I'm already broken. He broke me the moment we kissed each other. Nothing has been the same since.

"Don't give Jax any shit, okay? There's nothing between us. Besides, he's with someone, so you know, I kind of have to get him back home to his girlfriend in one piece."

"Girlfriend?"

She looked up at him.

"Yes, girlfriend. There was never any need for you to get all possessive over me."

"I did not get possessive."

"No? What do you call dragging me into the throne room and telling me I'm yours, then?"

He folded his arms across his chest, expression dark.

"You are mine."

75

She rolled her eyes. It was as if her confession hadn't happened. It had though. She felt things for the angel in front of her. Things she should never feel. It didn't even matter to her anymore that he was the Devil. He was the man she wanted in her bed, in her life and worst of all, in her heart.

"Are you going to behave?"

He looked sullen for a moment but nodded. She pulled away from the door and adjusted his shirt so it wasn't bunched up where she'd tugged at it. She stopped short of taking his hand even though a part of her wanted to.

She opened the door, taking a breath before striding towards Jax. He was still standing in the same place.

"Cadmi... what's going on?"

"We just needed to have a conversation. It's fine. Come with me."

She took his arm and pulled him along before opening the door to the living room. She made Jax sit down on the sofa. Lucifer had followed along behind. He stood a way off with his hands folded behind his back, his expression neutral. She sat down next to Jax.

"Does he know why I sent you here?" Jax asked.

"Not entirely no. I shouldn't have even told you."

"Keeping a secret like that can't have been easy."

She glanced back at Lucifer. His posture was stiff, eyes dark with repressed emotion. There was no doubt in her mind, he did not like her being close to Jax despite her assurance that there was nothing between them. Then again, she doubted Lucifer would be happy seeing her near any other man.

"It doesn't matter. What we need to discuss is how we're going to get home."

"Because no one is getting out of Hell right now."

"How did you even know about that?"

Jax shrugged, adjusting his t-shirt. He was in pyjamas. She looked down at her watch. It was midnight back on Earth.

"Rumours."

"And how did you even send me here in the first place? You don't have that type of power."

"Alistair."

"You involved him in this? Are you crazy? You know that could've got back to my father."

Jax is a fucking idiot.

This was turning into the biggest mess. How was she ever going to explain any of this to her father when she returned home? He was going to be mad. Mad and disappointed yet again.

"I didn't involve him. It wasn't as if I was opening the gates. It didn't involve blood magic. Alistair knows more about portals than anyone else. All he did was tell me how. No questions asked."

"Portal magic is dangerous if misused, you know that more than anyone."

"You managed to bring me here."

She put her head in her hands.

"It wasn't a portal. That was more like a summoning, which by the way, was not my intention. I was trying to create a gateway to Earth."

"A gateway?"

She stood up, staring down at Jax. This conversation was exhausting and learning he'd involved someone else made it all the more frustrating.

"Yes, it's all in this book. I'll show you when we've both got some sleep. You must be tired."

Mall came in and spoke softly to Lucifer for a moment. He nodded. She made her way over to Jax and Candace.

"If you'd like to come with me, I have a room prepared for you," she said.

Jax looked up at Candace, his eyes questioning. She nodded her head. He was perfectly safe with Mall.

"Right," he said, standing. "Sleep is wise, you did kind of wake me up. Sam is going to be pissed."

"You can deal with that when we get home or blame me. Whatever works," Candace said.

Jax left with Mall, leaving her alone with Lucifer. She wanted to collapse. The spellcasting had taken it out of her, not to mention suddenly having to deal with Jax being here.

She made her way around the sofa, coming to a halt in front of him. Lucifer stared down at her with an unreadable expression. She took his hand.

"Bed?"

He frowned.

"You want me to come with you?"

"If you're not busy. Do I have to ask nicely?"

He smiled a little, shaking his head. She tugged him into the bedroom before letting go of his hand. She strolled into the walk-in wardrobe, changing into something more comfortable. A plain t-shirt and sleep shorts.

When she walked back out, he was lying in his bed, tucked under the covers. She crawled in next to him, feeling the weight of the world sitting on her shoulders.

"Are you going to insist I hold you again?" he asked.

"You don't have to. I'm sorry I forced you last time."

His arm shot out, pulling her to him. He wrapped his arms around her, burying his face in her red hair.

"I like holding you," he whispered.

Her heart did a somersault in her chest.

If that's not the sweetest thing he's ever said to me, then I don't know what is.

Pulling away, she stared up into his mesmerising dark eyes. They were the sort of eyes she could get lost in forever. Perhaps it was just because she loved staring at them that she felt that way. She had it bad for Lucifer. So bad that she would leave a piece of herself here with him when she left.

Her eyes found his mouth.

"All I can think about right now is kissing you," she whispered, reaching up and brushing her fingers across his jaw.

"Are you asking for permission?"

"No. I want it to be just a kiss and nothing else."

He cupped the back of her head, pulling her into him. Their lips met with the gentlest of touches.

"I'm not going to push you anymore. No matter how much I want you. But you'll always be mine, Candace. Even when you return to Earth."

She pressed her mouth more firmly on his, wanting so much more than just a simple kiss from him. His words in her head made it hard for her to resist him.

I think I was yours from the moment I landed on you, Lucifer.

Her hand curled into his hair, tugging at the strands. He groaned, pressing her closer. Even if she wanted this to go further, it couldn't. She pulled away from him, regret filling her heart.

"You know I wish things could be different, don't you?"

"You won't explain it, so how would I know what you wish?"

"I wish I had a choice and if I had a choice, then I'd let you ruin me. I'd let you drown me like I want you to. I'd let all of this happen without question because all I want is right here in front of me."

She hid her face in his chest, unable to take the look in his eyes. There was something about the angel which made her want to admit all her secrets. All the reasons why she couldn't be with him. Perhaps he would try to save her, but she was resigned to it. If she didn't go back, she'd never forgive herself. Her chance at happiness was slipping away and yet there was absolutely nothing she could do to stop it.

"What's between us is more than just about sex to you?" he asked.

"I thought I'd already made that clear. It doesn't matter if it's only sex to you. I don't expect anything else."

There was a long moment of silence which made her wonder if she'd said the right thing.

"It's not just sex. I want every part of you. You are mine to ruin. Only mine."

Her heart stopped dead in her chest.

Lucifer wants all of me? Doesn't he know he already has that? Fuck. Fuck. Fuck.

Her resolve was shot to pieces.

She was going to let him ruin her.

Completely.

Chapter Eleven

*I*t took two weeks for Candace and Jax to find a solution to their predicament. She stopped counting how many failed attempts. Jax had more knowledge than she did which meant they didn't have any more accidents.

She'd managed to keep him from discovering she had feelings for the Devil. It didn't stop Lucifer getting in bed with her almost every time she caught some sleep. Kissing turned to teasing and teasing to touching, but it never went further. It was driving her crazy. The force of their pent-up desire for each other was going to explode.

"I know what we're missing," Jax said.

"What?"

"Divine power."

She stared at her best friend with wide eyes.

"And how do you think we're going to get that? Walk up to God and be like — hey, we want out of Hell, fancy lending us some of your juice?"

He rolled his eyes, shaking his head.

"You're forgetting we have divine power right here."

"Wait, you mean Lucifer?"

"He is an angel, Cadmi."

She sat back, drumming her fingers on the arm of the sofa. Jax was right. It didn't sit well with her, but he was right.

"Fine, but I'll ask him."

"Not even going to argue that point with you. He doesn't like me very much."

She grinned. Despite knowing Jax had a girlfriend, Lucifer didn't like how close they were. Jax was her only real childhood friend. He was special to her. Knew almost everything about her. Lucifer just had to suck it up no matter how possessive he was of her.

"I don't think he likes many people to be honest."

"He likes you."

Yeah, well, he cares for me in a way Jax doesn't know about and cannot ever discover.

"He didn't at first. You know I like to speak my mind. That grated on him, but now, I guess we found some common ground."

They were both caged by family duty. Freedom wasn't within their reach. In that respect, they were the same. It's only that Lucifer didn't know the extent of her duty to her family.

"Well, sooner rather than later. I need to get home to Sam."

"I know."

Her heart sank. Her time with Lucifer was almost up and she had so many regrets. Why hadn't she made the most of it? There was no use thinking about that now.

"I'll ask him when he's done in the throne room," she continued. "I can't go interrupting him."

"Oh yeah, well, I'm going to catch some shut eye in the meantime."

He got up, ruffling her hair.

"Say, you haven't changed your hair since I've been down here. That's not like you."

She flushed, unable to help herself. She'd taken Lucifer's words to heart. The only reason she'd change her hair colour is if she gave into him.

"I've been preoccupied."

"Well, true. Still, I'd love to know what colour you're going to pick when you go confront Gallian."

"Don't remind me."

She was not looking forward to seeing her father and explaining where she'd been. Jax grinned before he strolled away, leaving her alone. She picked herself up and shuffled into Lucifer's bedroom. She had no idea how long he'd be.

Slumping down on the bed, she groaned. How was she going to word this? Would he even help them? He didn't want her to leave. He hadn't exactly voiced it, but it wasn't hard for her to guess. There was nothing for it but to just be straight with him about it.

She sat up. Her heart thumped uncomfortably in her chest. Jax's reminder about her hair stuck out in her mind. Sliding off the bed, she went over to the mirror. It took a minute, but her hair changed from fire red to so blonde it was almost white.

"This is me," she whispered.

It had been so long, she'd forgotten what she looked like with it. Her violet eyes were stark against the background of her light hair.

He wants to see the real me. Is it crazy I want to show him? If I have to leave, then I can't go without knowing.

She turned away from the mirror, going into the walk-in wardrobe. She stripped out of all her clothes, selecting a short black silk robe. She shrugged it on and tied the belt around her waist tightly.

She stepped back out into the bedroom just as the doors on the other side opened. Lucifer's eyes met hers. There was absolutely no going back now. And she really didn't want to. What she wanted was the angel in front of her.

"You're here," she said.

"Yes. Were you waiting?"

She took a few steps towards him.

"I have to ask you something, but I don't really want to because it means everything ends and I..."

He took a step towards her then froze. His eyes roamed over her, landing on her hair.

"Is that...?"

She closed the distance between them, staring up at him. He reached out, wrapping a strand of her hair around his fingers. Her breath hitched.

What is he thinking? He's told me so many times he wants me to give into him, but now it's happening, I don't know if it's truly what he desires.

"You wanted to see the real me."

"Does this mean what I think it does?"

She swallowed, needing a moment before she answered him.

"Yes."

"You're beautiful," he whispered.

Her heart threatened to break there and then. The tenderness in his expression left her emotions in a mess at her feet. And all she wanted was to drown in him forever. She went up on her tiptoes, pressing a hard kiss to his mouth. His arms came about her, keeping her pinned to his chest.

"Ask me what you need to. I need to know. I won't take you until you do."

Releasing his mouth, her eyes met his. Her heart thundered in her ears. She'd heard him correctly. This was going to happen.

"Jax is sure he can cast the right spell, but we need... you."

His eyes narrowed.

"Me?"

"Well, it's more that we need divine power to complete it. So, yes, you."

"If that's what you need, then so be it."

What? He's not even going to ask why or how?

"I thought you'd be a bit more reluctant to help us since it means I have to go home."

"You forget, if you do this, then there's a way out of Hell and that will shut my subjects up."

He was right. It would benefit him. But she didn't want to think about any of that. She didn't want to think about how much it would break her heart when she left.

No. Now all I want is him and I for however long I have left.

"Lucifer... I know you didn't ask, but my answer this time is yes."

He released her, looking down at what she was wearing.

"Do you have anything on underneath that?"

"No."

His eyes darkened. His tongue ran over his bottom lip. It made her pulse quicken. A shiver ran down her spine. It occurred to her they'd never seen each other naked before. She reached up, flipping open the buttons on his shirt. He didn't stop her when she tugged it off his shoulders.

Oh, holy fuck.

He was so perfect it made her head spin. She ran her hand down his chest.

"Well, shit," she breathed.

"Are you quite done admiring me?"

Her eyes snapped up to his. There was amusement in his expression.

84

"I don't think I'll ever be done admiring you."

He put his hands on her shoulders, backing her towards the bed. When the backs of her calves hit it, they stopped. She blinked and then, he was only clad in boxers. It was still a little weird when he changed his clothes at will, but she was getting used to it.

His fingers went to the belt of her robe, untying it slowly. Her hands shook.

What if he doesn't like what he sees? What if he decides he doesn't want this any longer?

She tried to shush her ridiculous thoughts.

When he slipped it off her shoulders, it fell into a pool at her feet. She couldn't look at him, but she heard the sharp intake of his breath. His fingers tucked under her chin, forcing her face upwards. His eyes were dark with desire, lust, want, need. He pressed his mouth to hers, his hands running down her bare back.

"Perfect. All of you is perfect."

Her hands curled around his back, pulling him closer. She could feel his chest brushing against hers. It sent tingles down her spine. She'd wanted Lucifer from the moment they'd met. Giving in felt right. Having him against her felt perfect. Two months of denying herself was too much.

He pressed her down on the bed, covering her with his body. The heat between them spiked as his fingers brushed down her sides. He released her mouth, pressing kisses to her collarbone.

"Lucifer," she whimpered.

"Mmm, are you impatient after denying me for so long?"

He pressed her legs open, settling in between them. His fingers trailed up her inner thighs. She arched up against him.

"Yes. Aren't you?"

His eyes glittered with mischief.

"I want to take my time, savour each moment, each kiss, each touch." Fingers trailed up her sides with each word. "You're mine. Every inch of you."

Even if that's what he wanted, she most definitely didn't. All she could think about was him inside her.

"You can take your time later. No teasing... please."

Her fingers hooked into the waistband of his boxers. His smile turned wicked, but he didn't stop her as she relieved him of the final barrier between them.

He is stunning. I know he's an angel, but really, it should be illegal to be that attractive.

Curling her fingers into his hair, she tugged him down so she could kiss him. His fingers ran up her inner thighs again, inching them open further. He gripped her hips, pressing up against her sex. He groaned into her mouth.

"Fuck, you're so hot and wet. I need to feel you all over me, right now."

Lucifer, please. I can't take it. I ache for you.

In one swift movement, he pressed inside her. Her fingers dug into his back. All her focus was on where their bodies joined together. It was everything and more. Every inch he gave her sent a wave of pleasure rushing over her entire body. She was sure this had something to do with him being an angel, but she didn't care. She turned her face from his, needing to take a breath.

"Fuck," she whispered.

He buried his face in her neck, pressing hot kisses to her skin. He set a slow, almost gentle pace, pressing deeper with each stroke. It seemed so at odds with his brutal nature and their explosive desire for each other. Yet, it felt right to her.

Something had changed between them that first night she'd asked him to stay with her.

He released one of her hips, grabbing her hand, he pressed it down next to them, entwining her fingers with his. His other hand brushed up her side before he cupped her face, staring down at her with those mesmerising eyes of his.

"This is worth every second I've spent longing for you," he said.

He saved her answering him. Pressing his mouth to hers, passion ignited between them. His pace quickened. She hooked a leg around his, drawing him closer. She felt it everywhere. Him. His hands on her skin. The power he exuded washed over her, trailing along her skin like electricity.

Harder. I want more. I want all of you. I need everything.

She matched his movements, both lost in each other as he gave her exactly what she'd asked for. She'd never felt as close to anyone as she did to Lucifer in that moment.

Crying out, her fingers dug into his back when she started to feel the familiar stirrings of her impending climax. It was if his hands were running down every inch of her skin. Jolts ran down her spine until she felt them right in her core.

"That's it, let go," he whispered, his mouth close to her ear.

It was like something snapped inside her. She cried out his name, shaking and trembling as the intense pleasure tore through her. His pace didn't slow, if anything he pounded into her faster, harder and every stroke sent a new wave across her core. Her cries of pleasure echoed through the room, quite unable to hold back as the dam broke entirely. He grunted, his hand tightening in hers when he lost control too.

It was a long while before she fought her way back through the fog of ecstasy he'd brought on. She smiled, closing her eyes. He was still pinning her to the bed with his body, but she didn't care. It was perfect. So perfect she wanted to experience it all over again. She wasn't ready to go home at all. Not after the life altering sex she'd just had.

"Candace," he said, his voice a little hoarse. "Stay with me."

Her eyes snapped to his. Her heart felt tight, constricting in her chest. Every part of her wanted so much for all of this to be different.

"Don't ask me to do that, please," she whispered.

Chapter Twelve

*L*ucifer stared down at the woman who utterly disarmed him. There were tears welling in her eyes. He hadn't meant to ask her to stay, but the words came tumbling out anyway.

His infatuation with her had turned into feelings. Raw, intense feelings that drove him crazy. Candace meant something to him. He never expected to want anyone, but he wanted all of her. He'd never needed anyone before, but he needed her. For the first time in millennia, he didn't care about his exile from Heaven nor his duty as the King of Hell. She gave him a small slice of happiness. This half witch, half fae girl with magic running in her veins. She was everything to him.

"I don't want to talk about the future," she continued. "I just want to be here with you, now. Can we do that?"

"Yes."

Denying her wasn't in him at that moment. He didn't want to fight with her again. He knew she belonged on Earth, but the selfish part of him wanted her here. With him. Always.

He rolled them over, so she was sitting on top of him. She flicked her long, blonde hair back behind her shoulders. Violet eyes stared down at him with tenderness and affection.

She isn't supposed to care for me. This was never meant to be anything but sex. She is mine, my little witch, and she doesn't know I am hers.

He could've been brutal, pinned her down and fucked her until she couldn't take it any longer. However, Mall's warning still rang in his ears every time his temper flared.

Be gentle with her.

It was that gentleness he'd shown which had led them to this moment.

"Are you going to ride me?" he asked in a low voice.

"Is that what you want?"

He grinned. She trailed a finger down his chest. He caught one of her hands, bringing it to his lips. He placed a kiss on each of her fingertips.

"I want to watch you pleasure yourself at my expense."

A flush rose up her neck. There was a faint pink tinge to her cheeks. She looked away, almost hiding her face in her hair.

"Lucifer..."

His smile widened at her embarrassment.

Oh, she's not getting out of this that easily.

He pulled her towards him by her hand, only letting go so he could cup her breast. They were perfect handfuls. He ran a thumb over her nipple before replacing it with his mouth. She cried out, wriggling on him. He gripped her hip, encouraging her to rise and fall. He growled against her skin. Her heat was intoxicating. She arched her back, her hand falling on his chest to steady herself. He released her when she moved faster. She bit her lip, looking down at him with lust filled eyes.

She has no idea how sexy that is. I want to bite that lip.

"That's right fuck me just like you've longed to do all this time."

She said nothing, closing her eyes and tipping her head back. She really was something else. Now he'd felt her, there was no going back between them. He shifted, sitting up with her still in his lap. She wrapped her arms around his neck, tugging him closer.

"I don't want to leave you," she whispered. "Despite all our fights and arguments, I'm happiest with you."

She rose and fell faster, her breath coming harder.

"Neither of us belong in each other's worlds," he said, running his fingers down her back.

"And yet, I'm still yours."

She kissed him. His hand fell in between them, encouraging her to let go again. And they held each other for the longest time when the aftershocks had faded. Their short time together almost at an end. Lucifer decided then and there, he would find a way to have her here again.

He wasn't ready to let the woman in his arms go.

Not now.

Not ever.

Lucifer didn't like Candace's friend. Despite her reassurances there was nothing between them, he saw the way Jaxon looked at her.

She's blind to his adoration. Girlfriend or not, that boy's affection is not platonic by any stretch of the imagination.

He watched the two of them in deep conversation. They'd almost finished preparing what they needed to, in order to open the gateway. He couldn't deny they needed the boy's magic ability. Candace's heritage made her magic unique, but as she'd told him, it was not necessarily a good thing.

She looked up at him, smiling. It gave him a strange feeling inside.

Why do I care for her this way? Why does one single look make me want to get on my knees and plead with her to stay?

She made him weak, but he couldn't hate her for it. He only felt affection for the woman who was leaving him behind.

She left Jaxon's side and came over to him, placing a hand on his arm. The memory of her naked body curled around his as she slept assaulted his senses. She'd looked so peaceful. Her touch made him harden instantly.

Fuck. I want her again. I want her all the time.

"Jax is ready."

"Are you?"

She looked up at him with wide eyes.

"You know I'll never be ready," she replied, her voice low. "Last night was more than I could've ever asked for."

She dropped her hand, glancing at Jaxon, but he wasn't looking over at them. He narrowed his eyes. She was keeping their relationship a secret from that boy.

"Are you really concerned about him knowing?"

"It isn't any of his business."

He reached up, gripped her face and forced her to look at him. Why would she keep something like this from someone she shared everything with? He knew very well they'd known each other since they were children and Candace had confided all of her secrets to him.

"No?"

"Lucifer..."

She tried to look at Jaxon again, but he held her still. She wasn't getting away from him that easily. He'd make her tell him the truth.

"Are you ashamed?"

Her eyes snapped back to his, confusion and anger in her expression.

"What? No, of course not."

His eyes narrowed further. Tugging her closer, he stared down at those violet eyes which haunted his every moment.

She drives me crazy with her stubborn nature.

"I don't believe you."

"You don't have to."

She grabbed his hand, trying to tug it away from her face. His temper flared. She was walking on thin ice with him.

"Lying to me only ends one way."

"Stop it," she hissed.

"The truth, Candace. I want the truth."

She glared at him, clamping her mouth shut. If she was going to play this game with him, then so be it.

She only has herself to blame.

He dropped her face, gripping her arm instead.

"Excuse me, Candace and I need a word in private."

He didn't wait for a response from either of them. He dragged her from the room despite her protests.

"Lucifer, get off!"

"You know the rules. You're being disobedient."

"I am not."

When they reached his bedroom, he tugged her over to the desk.

"Kneel."

"What the fuck? No. Let go of me."

Her refusal made the leash he had on his temper snap completely. He pressed her back against the desk, pinning her body to it with his own. He took both her arms, twisting them behind her back. He used his power to keep them tied behind her. She stared up at him, eyes wide with shock and confusion.

"What the fuck are you doing?"

She struggled against the invisible bonds.

"Teaching you a lesson. One you'll not likely forget."

"Lucifer, stop this."

"You only had to tell me the truth, but no, that's too hard for you to manage."

He clicked his fingers and she was naked before him the next moment. She looked down at herself. When her eyes met his again, they were blazing with anger.

"The truth? The fucking truth? I don't want people's judgement, especially not his. Do you know what he'll say? What anyone will say if they find out I've been with the Devil? Do you imagine they will look at me with anything but disgust for allowing you to touch me? Do you? No, because you don't fucking care. You take what you want without consequence."

Her words only fuelled his rage. Did their night together mean nothing to her? Hadn't he shown her how he felt?

I asked her to stay for fuck's sake. Surely she should know I want her, need her.

Why did she even care what people thought? Humans were like sheep. They'd been led to believe he was evil. Is this how she really felt about the two of them?

"I should leave you here, tied up and naked because it's no less than you deserve. Is that what you think? Does it disgust you that we've fucked? That I've touched every inch of your body and given you exactly what you craved?"

"No! Don't you understand? I fucking care about you. All I want is you. I must be crazy for needing everything about you like I need fucking air. I swear if you don't fuck me right now, I might lose my mind completely."

Fuck. She doesn't half make me so crazy for her.

She'd never been disgusted by him. He knew that, but he still didn't understand why other people's opinions mattered. All that mattered was what was between them.

He wasn't going to hold back. She demanded he fuck her.

He kissed her, his hands tangled in her hair which she'd changed to blue before she'd left his room yesterday. She kissed him back with just as much ferocity.

He sat her on the desk, tearing open his trousers and freeing his cock. He pressed into her heated sex, groaning. She was so wet. He gripped her hips, pounding into her with no mercy.

She makes me so fucking angry. I want to punish her. To make her understand she is mine. My little witch. Mine.

"Fuck, Lucifer, fuck me harder," she groaned.

Her words sent him into a frenzy. Her arms were still bound, but he didn't care at that moment. All he could think about was sending them both into oblivion. Perhaps they'd never come back from it. It occurred to him he didn't want to. He wanted to drown in her intoxicating scent. Drown in his need for her.

"Please, fuck, more," she whispered

Slamming into her with so much force, he was sure she'd end up with bruises, she cried out. Her climax raced through her body like wildfire. He could feel it everywhere. And he couldn't hold back, grunting as his own end tore through him.

They were both panting when their trembling subsided. He released the hold on her arms. She wrapped them around him, leaning her head on his shoulder.

"Screw you," she whispered. "Why do you do this to me?"

"You know why."

"Why do I want you so much?"

"Only you can answer that." Her arms around him tightened. "You can hate me all you want, Candace, it changes nothing. You are mine."

"I don't hate you."

She pulled away, cupping his cheek with one hand. It took a concerted effort on his part not to lean into her touch.

"You mean more to me then you know, but I need to go home."

He pulled away, clicking his fingers. She was dressed again and his clothing was no longer in disarray. She shoved off the desk, taking his hand and entwining her fingers in his. He raised an eyebrow.

"Just let me hold your hand," she said.

It made him smile just a little. He tugged her along until they reached the room where they were going to create the gateway. She stopped him from going in. Pressing him up against the wall, she kissed him like she was drowning in him. He held her close. When she pulled away, her face was flushed.

"I couldn't leave without doing that one last time," she said.

"A goodbye kiss?"

"I think you just gave me a goodbye fuck."

He chuckled, kissing her again. This wasn't goodbye, but he refrained from saying so. He was going to get her back no matter what.

They walked back into the room. Jaxon raised his eyebrows at Candace, but she shook her head.

"It's time," she said.

He nodded. The two of them got to work drawing an intricate pentagram within a circle. When they were done, she beckoned him over. He stood just outside the circle next to her. Jaxon began to speak in Latin. It was a low chant.

Lucifer put his hand out, a soft glowing ball of power appeared in his palm. He sent it towards the bowl by Jaxon's feet when the witch nodded to him.

The circle began to shimmer with a purple light. It swirled for several long minutes before clearing. They could all see the streets of London reflected back at them.

"It worked," Jaxon said.

Lucifer looked at Candace. Her eyes were brimming with tears. He brushed his fingers against hers. Her head snapped up, violet eyes full of turmoil.

"I don't want to go," she whispered. "I don't want my fate."

The sight of her and her words almost broke him. She'd said all she wanted was him. All he wanted was her. And there was nothing he could do right now which would make the situation any easier.

"Come on, Cadmi, it's time," Jaxon said.

"Okay," she said, her voice cracking on the word.

She turned away, reaching out and taking Jaxon's hand. The two of them stepped up to the newly created portal. Before she stepped in, she looked back at him. Tears fell down her cheeks unheeded.

"Goodbye," she whispered.

Then the woman who'd stolen everything from him walked through the portal and out of his life.

And he couldn't understand why it made his heart ache so much.

Chapter Thirteen

andace stepped out onto the dark street with Jax. Her cheeks were wet with tears. She brushed them away with her sleeve, but her eyes were still streaming.

What have I done?

"Cadmi?"

"Yes?" she sniffled.

"What's wrong?"

She didn't look at him. She wanted to curl up in bed and shut out the world.

"Nothing."

He grabbed her by the arms, turning her to face him.

"Why are you crying?"

"Just leave it, Jax. I'm going home."

She tried to pull away, but he held fast.

"Is it about him? What happened between the two of you?"

Lucifer.

Her heart ached with an intensity that almost crippled her.

"Nothing. I don't want to talk about it. I'll call you tomorrow."

She tore away from him, walking quickly down the street.

"Cadmi!"

"Don't call me that."

She didn't turn back to look at him. In the next street over, she realised they'd landed not far from her flat. It was the one small mercy in all of this.

Letting herself in a few minutes later, she locked the door and went straight into her bedroom. She ripped off her clothes and crawled into bed, sobbing for all she was worth.

Fuck. Damn it. Why? Why? Why do I feel like this? Why is leaving him so fucking heartbreaking?

She knew the answers to those questions. Admitting it to herself was a whole different ball game. The weight of her feelings crashed down on her. Burrowing deeper in the covers, she clutched her knees to her chest. The ache she felt there was unending.

Fuck. I love him. I'm in love with the Devil.

And nothing she could say or do would change that fact.

It was her own stupid fault for sleeping with him. For allowing herself to indulge in her feelings for him. How would she face anyone now? She was in love with someone the world considered evil. He wasn't evil to her. Brutal maybe, but Lucifer had been gentle with her too. She'd seen a side of him she knew no one else got to witness.

She cried harder, her sobs echoing in her ears.

Why didn't I just stay with him like he asked me to?

She could've. No one but Jax would've known. Running away and staying with Lucifer was cowardly. Duty came first. Duty to her family.

She awoke with a jolt, the sunlight streaming in through the open curtains. She groaned, pulling the covers over her eyes. Reaching out, she found the bed empty. She sat up. Lucifer wasn't there.

This isn't Hell. This is home. Shit.

She hadn't seen daylight in two months, having got used to living in perpetual darkness down in Hell. They had electric lights, but it wasn't the same.

She hauled herself out of bed and jumped in the shower. A wave of pain shot through her heart. She couldn't help dissolving into another fit of sobs.

She got out when they finally abated, dressing and going through into her open plan living room. Her mail was piled up by the front door along with her purse. Jax must've posted it through the front door. She rifled through it, finding her phone. It was dead.

She picked up the mail, dumping it on the kitchen counter and stuck her phone on charge. Next, she threw out all the out of date food from her fridge, freezer and then the cupboards just for something to do.

When she turned her phone back on, it was flooded with texts and voicemails.

She listened to the voicemails, grimacing when she realised most of them were from her father.

"Candace, where are you? Why did I have to hear it from Jax that you've not been home in days?"

Because I was in Hell, Dad.

"Are you acting up again? Is this your idea of punishing me? I've told you a thousand times I did not want to make such a deal with your life. You are my only child, but I had no choice. Is this why you've run away? Is facing your duty so abhorrent to you?"

She deleted the rest of the messages without listening to them. There was no point. It was time she faced the music. She pulled on a coat, sticking her phone in her bag. She dropped by a cafe on the way for brunch before jumping on the Underground and making her way to Marylebone. Stuffing her headphones in her ears, she boarded a train to Oxford.

An hour and one taxi ride later, she stood outside her father's house. Gallian Highmore lived in an expensive townhouse. She'd grown up here but moved to London at eighteen to get away from the Grand Coven and their insufferable rules.

She let herself in, hung her coat up in the hall cupboard and kicked off her trainers. Her slippers were still sitting by the door. She stuffed her feet into them and trudged through into the kitchen. Her father would be in his study, but she might as well bring him a cup of tea.

When she'd made a teapot, complete with a little jug of milk, two teacups on saucers and the sugar bowl, she carried the tray upstairs and didn't bother knocking. Her father turned around at the sound of her barging into his study.

She put the tray down on a side table and poured two cups with sugar, setting them on his desk. She was about to sit down when her father moved and wrapped his arms around her. He held her whilst she stood stiffly in his embrace.

Um, what? He never offers me affection.

"Where have you been for two months, Candace?" he said, his voice a little tense.

"It's a long story, Dad."

"Do you have any idea how worried I've been? You disappeared without a trace."

She patted his back, unsure why he was still holding her.

"I know. I didn't have any way of contacting anyone. I'm sorry."

He released her, putting his hands on her shoulders and staring down at her. His brown hair was greying at the sides and his rust brown eyes were full of concern. He was at least half a head taller than her.

"Why did you leave?"

"It's not my fault. It's Jax... he sent me to Hell."

"He what?" Gallian stepped back, running a hand through his hair. "Does he have any idea how dangerous that is? Why on earth would he do such a thing?"

"Because he knows."

Her father gave her a sharp look.

"You told him?"

"How do you think he'd feel if I dropped off the face of the planet on my birthday? He's my best friend."

"That boy has always been infatuated with you."

She almost choked on her own breath. Jax wasn't infatuated with her. They cared about each other, but it had only ever been as friends. And he had Sam. They were happy, even if Sam didn't like her very much. Jax would never throw away their friendship over a girl.

"No, he's not."

"I'm going to have strong words with his mother."

"Dad, no. He made a mistake. He knows that."

Her father walked around the desk and sat back in his chair, taking the teacup and sipping at his tea. She slumped in the chair in front of the desk, looking at him with a tense expression.

"Why did you not return straight away?"

"I couldn't. When I got there, I discovered no one was allowed to leave. All the portals and the gates had been sealed. I've spent the past two months trying to get around that, but it was only when I accidentally summoned Jax that we were finally able to return home. I got back last night, so I came as soon as I could. I promise, Dad, I didn't do this to get out of anything. I know my duty."

"You summoned Jax to Hell? How did you stay alive down there?"

She stifled a sigh. How would she explain where exactly she'd been? She didn't need her father finding out about her and Lucifer.

"You know I can't do portal magic. It wasn't on purpose. And I stayed alive because I'm resourceful, besides, they appreciated my help in fixing what God did."

"What?"

"God sealed them in Hell, at least that's what Lu... I was told."

Her father's eyebrows drew together in a frown.

"Does it matter what happened? I'm back now and in time for my birthday."

"I'm still not happy with that boy for sending you there in the first place, but it's not a matter you need to concern yourself with. Your mother knows you've been missing."

It was the last thing she wanted to hear. Her mother was the reason her life wasn't her own. She picked up her teacup, taking a huge gulp before setting it back down.

"Why did you tell her?"

"How was I to know you'd return home before your birthday? I will speak to her. Preparations have been made in your absence. The ball will be held and you will go."

His expression told her everything. He was disappointed in her yet again. None of this had been her fault, but that never seemed to matter to him.

"I know, Dad. You don't have to look at me like that."

"And just how do you think I'm looking at you?"

This was a dangerous line of conversation. They'd argued over this so many times, she'd lost count. It always came back to the same thing. He'd never once told her he was proud of her nor made her feel like she was adequate.

"I can't do anything right in your eyes." She stood abruptly. "I've done everything you asked. I'm even giving up my life because of you and her, but that's not good enough for you. Do you think I want this? Chained in servitude for the rest of my existence. It's not my fault you had a secret affair with her nor that I was the product of it. Do you know what it's like to be scorned by both witches and fae just because I'm a half blood? No, because no one would dare say a bad word to the leader of the Grand Coven about his daughter."

The words tumbled out in a rush. After everything she'd been through in the last two months, her ability to keep her mouth shut was shot to pieces. She'd been fine with all of it until she'd met Lucifer. Met him, fought with him, had mind-blowing sex with him and worst of all, fallen in love with him. Now, it all made her angry.

She paced away, clenching her fists.

"Candace, do you really believe that?"

"What else am I supposed to believe when all you do is tell me how much I've disappointed you? I know when you look at me you see her."

The seconds of silence ticked by. Her heart was already shattered. It broke the moment she left Hell. What did it matter if her father never gave her the love she desperately craved from him? She'd learnt long ago there was no use arguing with Gallian Highmore. No use pleading with him.

"I'm going back to London. I only came to tell you I'm home."

"Candace..."

"Don't, Dad. There's nothing to say."

She walked out of his office, tears threatening to spill down her cheeks. There was only one thing she wanted to do. Drown herself in booze and not think for a while. Not remember Lucifer's hands on her or his mesmerising dark eyes. Nor think about her conversation with her father or her fate. All of it broke her heart further.

She didn't want to go to ObliVion and run into her mother's lackey who always seemed to take up permanent residence there. No, she'd go somewhere else away from humans. Away from witches. There was only one place they rarely ventured where she could drown her sorrows and it wouldn't get back to her father.

Fright Night.

Chapter Fourteen

*D*arkness had fallen by the time she arrived back in London and made her way to Soho. Trudging down the steps into the basement bar, she didn't bother checking her coat. She sat down on one of the bar stools and eyed the bartender who was serving someone else. It wasn't particularly busy this early, but she was glad of that.

"You look like shit. Bad day?"

She glanced up. Neave was leaning against the bar, grinning.

"Bad everything," she replied rolling her eyes. "Just give me something strong."

She'd been in the bar quite often and had gotten to know the vampire who owned it. She didn't much mind them, unlike her witch counterparts. It was a centuries old hatred which she thought was idiotic.

Neave moved away for a moment, selecting an expensive bottle of scotch.

"Is this the type of thing you're looking for?" the vampire asked.

"Sure."

The cost didn't bother her. It was her father's money. What did she care how much she spent of it? Especially after today. Neave poured some into a whisky tumbler and slid it across to her. She took a sip, grimacing a little. It was strong and burnt on the way down.

"I'll just leave the bottle here. I know you're good for it."

The vampire smiled before walking away to serve another customer. Pulling out her phone, she fired off a quick text to Jax.

Just a warning… Dad's pissed at you.

A few moments later, a reply came.

Where are you?

Drinking myself into an early grave.

That bad?

Worse, but don't worry about it. I'll deal.

We need to talk about what happened in Hell.

She stared down at her phone. There was no way she was having that conversation with Jax. She tucked it back in her bag. He could just wait.

Taking another sip of scotch, she sighed. Drinking alone. This was a new low, even for her. She usually did this with Jax, but she knew he needed to spend time with Sam and she didn't particularly want to have it out with him about Lucifer.

Why the fuck am I thinking about him again?

The pain in her chest was unbearable.

Picking up the tumbler, she downed the rest of it. Her father would scold her for drinking a single malt in such a way, but she didn't give a shit right then. She poured herself some more and sipped at it.

"Didn't expect to see you in here," came a voice she recognised.

She looked over at the dark-haired witch who took a seat next to her.

"I could say the same of you."

Alistair grinned, tipping an imaginary hat at her.

They'd known each other a long time.

Alistair had always been a bit of a lady's man. His conquests included Candace herself. One drunken night not long after she'd moved to London, she'd been out clubbing with him and Jax. One thing led to another and she'd ended up back at his. Both of them agreed never to mention it again. It was one of the few things she swore she'd never tell Jax about.

She was glad he'd finally settled down with someone. Although, she knew very well his mother completely disapproved of his choice. She'd been there the day the Grand Coven had sentenced Ophelia. Stripped of your magic and permanently frozen in time was not a fate she wished on anyone.

"How's Grace?" she asked.

"Oh, she's fine. Still refusing to entertain the idea of marriage, but I'm sure she'll come around in her own time."

She chuckled, indicating to Neave to get them another tumbler. The vampire picked up a glass and slid it down the bar. Candace caught it and poured a scotch for Alistair.

"You know it's funny seeing you all smitten with a girl."

"Jealous, are we? You had your chance."

He gave her a wink, taking a sip of whisky.

"And now I suddenly remember why I never wanted a repeat of that incident."

He knocked his shoulder into hers.

"Say, why are you here alone instead of with Jax?"

She should've known he'd ask about that.

"I need to talk to you about something. This has to stay between us."

She turned to him, her expression serious. He raised an eyebrow but nodded.

"Did Jax ask you how to create a portal to Hell and did you help him with it?"

He looked down at his drink for a moment before sighing and running a hand through his hair.

"He asked me some questions, but I don't know why he wanted to know. What's this about?"

"He sent me to Hell and I couldn't get back for two months. Don't worry, I'm fine, but my dad is pissed off for obvious reasons. And I really don't want you getting in the crosshairs for being inadvertently involved."

She took another sip of whisky. Warning him felt like the right thing to do.

"I'm going to chuck that idiot in the Thames. Wait, so the rumours were true? Hell was really sealed off? Shit. I mean after all that crap with the Darkness last year, I thought things had been too quiet on that front."

"The Darkness?"

"Oh well, yeah. You must've been in Oxford when it happened. It was the end-of-the-world shit involving pretty much all of us. It was crazy. I've never seen so many angels and who'd have thought I'd actually get to see the Devil up close."

105

Her heart thumped in her chest at the mention of his name. Was this what he'd been talking about the day they'd met?

"Lucifer?"

He eyed her for a moment, frowning a little.

"Yes. I didn't speak to him, but he got into this huge fight with Azrael, you know, the Archangel of Death and then Michael turned up with Gabriel and Raphael. Also, in some crazy twist, Michael is actually Lukas' father. So, Azrael had to kill his own girlfriend to stop the Darkness, but it's all good. God brought her back to life and they live up in Heaven now."

She stared at Alistair with wide eyes. *What the actual fuck?* She tried to process everything he'd told her.

"What exactly was the Darkness?"

"God's wrath, though really, it was his punishment for Azrael siding with Lucifer in the war in Heaven on top of his exile. I'm just glad that's all over. I mean, if the world had ended, it would've sucked."

Her heart wrenched again.

Lucifer. It can't be easy for him knowing he's still exiled when his fellow angel had been allowed to go home.

All she wanted to do was wrap her arms around him. Tell him it was okay and she was here for him now. She couldn't do any of those things. He was in Hell and she was back on Earth where she belonged.

"Shit. Can't believe I knew nothing about this."

"Say, why are you so interested in it anyway?"

"Oh, it's just something he said when I was in Hell."

She slapped a hand over her mouth. It had slipped out without her realising.

"Who said?"

Alistair had always been discerning even if he was constantly making crude jokes and talking about himself like he was the best thing since sliced bread. He was smart, powerful and she always went to him when she needed help with magic. They were pretty close friends.

"Lucifer," she mumbled.

"You actually talked to him?"

"I spent two months with him, Alistair."

He grinned and winked at her.

"Oh, for fuck's sake, not like that."

It had been like that. She turned away, her face burning.

Damn it and now he's not going to drop it either. Shit. Why did I have to open my stupid mouth?

"You've gone up in my estimation."

Her head whipped around.

"What?"

"Was it good? I mean I can imagine he's into some weird shit."

Trust him to say something like that.

"Oh god, please stop talking."

"Who's into weird shit?" Neave asked.

Candace jumped, looking up at the vampire who was leaning on the bar in front of them.

"Candace did the dirty with the Devil when she was in Hell."

"Alistair!"

Neave's eyebrows shot up.

"Damn, he's hot. I don't blame you for getting a piece of that."

She folded her arms across her chest.

"I did not sleep with Lucifer."

"Says the girl who's on first name terms with him," Alistair said, grinning.

She was going to kill him in a minute. Why did he have to tell Neave? No one was supposed to know.

"Look, if I find out either of you has blabbed this to anyone else, I will hunt you down. Got it?" She looked between the two of them. They both nodded. "Yes, it was amazing. Now, kindly drop this subject before I bash your heads together."

"I need details," Neave said. "You fucked the Devil. If he batted his eyes at me, I'd come running."

She bit the side of her mouth.

I'm not jealous. Not at all. Not one bit. Who the fuck am I kidding? I can't stand the thought of him with anyone else.

She couldn't expect him to be faithful to her. It wasn't like they were in a relationship and she'd left him. Her heart contracted for what felt like the hundredth time that day. She had to stop thinking about him.

"Neave, with all due respect, fuck off."

The vampire smiled wide, shrugged and walked away, hips swaying. Alistair turned to her.

"Sorry."

"It's okay, it's just complicated. Don't say anything to Jax. He doesn't know."

"So, this is another thing to go in the 'we'll never speak of this incident again' tank?"

She took another sip of whisky, twirling the tumbler around in her hand.

"It's just really fucked up."

"When is your life ever not fucked up?"

Yeah, well, that drunken incident between us also involved spilling all our secrets to each other.

She knew about his grandmother and her visions. How he was meant to be leader of his aunt's coven. And he knew what would happen on her birthday.

"Touché."

"Come on, Candace, if you want to talk about it, you know I won't give you any shit for it."

She threw back the second tumbler of whisky and poured another for both of them. The alcohol numbed her senses. What if she confided the truth? Would she feel better having it out in the open?

"Will you give me shit for it if I tell you I accidentally fell in love with the Devil when I've got two more weeks before my life pretty much ends?"

He knocked back his own glass, pouring another one.

"Fuck. Does he know?"

"Are you crazy? No. It was never meant to happen. None of it. Why do you think I'm in a bar drowning my sorrows by myself?"

He put a hand on her shoulder, giving it a squeeze.

"You can drink with me."

"Don't you have a girlfriend to go home to? Why are you in here anyway?"

He shrugged.

"Gavin wants something, but as you can see, he's not here yet."

She rolled her eyes. When were vampires ever on time?

"Getting dragged into vamp shit again? Lucky you. I thought you disliked them."

"Looks like it. I did, but after you go through the end of the world with them, kind of hard to keep being all 'I hate you so much', you know."

She grinned.

Well, I wouldn't know, but I can imagine.

She didn't much mind vampires. Neave was an all right sort and she'd met Gavin on a handful of occasions. It was hard not to run into the man who ran London when you hung out in the bar owned by his second in command.

"How's your goddaughter?"

He dug out his phone, scrolling through and showing her photos. Him and Luna in the park with Grace. Him making stupid faces at Luna. Grace showing Luna a picture book.

"You two will make awesome parents one day."

"Don't tell Aunty Grace that. She'll have another fit and say it's too soon. Luna stays with us during the full moon so Izz and Rex don't worry about her."

She smiled at him, reminded again how glad she was he'd found someone to settle down with. It also made her sad. Her life was such a mess. She downed another whisky, feeling the burn again on the way down. If only she could stop thinking about the Devil for one minute, things might be easier. She knew she'd have no such luck.

I miss him already. I want him so much it hurts. I'm an idiot. A huge fucking idiot.

How was she going to deal with being away from him when all her heart wanted was Lucifer? She wanted to see his mesmerising eyes staring down at her and that deliciously wicked smile of his. It'd barely been twenty-four hours. This was a nightmare. One she needed to end.

"I need to get so drunk I can't remember my name any more," she said.

Alistair poured her another whisky, clinking his glass against hers.

"Bottoms up then."

Chapter Fifteen

Candace walked up the drive towards the huge mansion. She hated the dress that had been picked out for her. It was blue, skin tight with a long slit up the side, far too revealing and not something she'd ever pick out for herself. She couldn't help thinking that Lucifer would've loved to have seen her in this. She shook herself mentally.

Stop thinking about him. Just stop.

She'd turned twenty-five today. It was meant to be a milestone, but it just meant her life was over as she knew it. She spent last night and the morning with her father. Neither of them mentioned their previous conversation.

The afternoon was given over to preparing for the ball her mother was holding. Her blonde hair was braided. Her make up perfectly applied. And now it was time for her to face her duty.

She was greeted by two guards at the door, who let her in with a nod. Walking through into the ornate ballroom, she felt a little awkward. Several prominent members of the fae milled around. It was quite a crowd, but her mother's balls always attracted attention.

There was a group of girls nearby, looking her up and down with disdain written all over their faces. She ignored them, taking a glass from a tray which a waiter was carrying around. She knocked it back in one.

I hate fae wine, but I need something to get me through this evening.

In the corner near the doors which led to the private household rooms, one of her mother's handmaidens waved to get her attention. She dumped her empty glass and walked over.

"It's time," Pervinca said.

"Fine, lead the way," Candace replied.

She followed Pervinca through the doors and into a long corridor. The handmaiden brought her up the stairs at the end and into a large room. There were a fair few fae milling around. Raoul stuck out like a sore thumb. *Arrogant dickhead.* She hated him with a burning passion. His predatory grin when his gaze fell on her made her skin crawl.

"Well, if it isn't our special guest," he said.

"Hello, Raoul. Not out harassing poor unsuspecting girls this evening?"

"And miss your debut. I think not."

She stuck her finger up at him and walked away, finding a sofa in the corner and throwing herself down on it. From here she could see the balcony where her mother would make her entrance. There were others in the room, but she didn't much feel like acknowledging or making conversation with them. She hadn't wanted to be here in the first place.

There was the sound of a harp followed by a cello. The doors to the balcony opened and out stepped Queen Gwilliana. Her white blonde hair intricately braided, violet eyes piercing. Her mauve dress flowed around her in waves of fabric. A silver crown of thorns perched on her head. Her entourage, including Raoul, stepped out behind her. The ballroom went deadly silent.

"My beloved subjects, it is an honour to see so many of you gathered this evening," the queen said.

Candace rolled her eyes. This speech was going to go on forever. Pervinca slipped into the room again, holding a beautifully intricate circlet of silver leaves woven together. She approached Candace.

"May I?" she asked.

Candace nodded, allowing the girl to place it on her head and rearrange her braids around it. The girl smiled, bowed her head and left when she was done. Candace tuned back into the queen's speech.

"This ball is to commemorate a very special day in our lives. Today is my daughter's birthday."

A collective gasp ran through the assembly of fae below.

That's right, no one knows she has a daughter.

Candace stood up, walking towards the doors where she'd face her people.

"It is my pleasure to introduce to you all Princess Cadmi."

She strode out and stood next to her mother. Her eyes scanned the crowd. There were looks of shock, but also ones of admiration.

Who'd have thought? I've spent half my life scorned by them and now they're looking at me like I'm royalty. Well, I guess I am now. Officially at least.

She noticed a very familiar figure standing close to the balcony. Shock ran through her. She bit down hard on the side of her cheek, unable to stop staring. Everything about this was wrong. So unbelievably fucking wrong.

What is he doing here?

Lucifer leant against a pillar close to the balcony listening to the fae queen drone on. His eyes snapped up to the doors when her name was mentioned.

Princess?

Candace walked out in a skin-tight blue dress. It made his blood pound in his ears.

Fuck. I want her.

Even if she hadn't been wearing such a revealing outfit, he'd have wanted her all the same.

The moment she saw him, she froze. Her violet eyes widening. He'd known she would be here, Mall had been keeping tabs on Candace, but to discover she was the fae queen's daughter was unexpected.

This is what she's been keeping from me. My little witch is a princess of the fae.

Now he could see them standing together, the resemblance was striking. Their eyes were the exact same shade, but Candace's still maintained an innocence which had long since faded in the queen's eyes. Gwilliana was centuries old.

"It has been necessary to keep my daughter from you, but now, she joins us in her rightful place by my side. She is the chosen one."

Chosen one?

He frowned. The fae were always cryptic with their words.

"The prophecy will come to pass."

And here we go again. More prophetic bullshit.

"She who is born under the two stars. She who belongs to two worlds. She who comes to you in darkness. She who comes to you in light. She will bring the dawn and cast out the night. She will restore you. She will be your sacrifice."

Just as I thought. Idiotic.

Candace's eyes were still on him. He wanted to know what she was thinking. It was clear she wasn't happy he was here. Not when she'd kept all of this from him. If this was what she meant by her duty, then it wasn't going to stand in the way of the two of them.

"I am honoured to inform you I have chosen her mate. Princess Cadmi will marry Prince Theodus of the Farlane clan. We have long since wished to bind our families together and today marks the first steps towards our happy union."

A tall fae male with long chestnut brown hair and a small silver crown of ivy woven together stepped out from the room behind the balcony. He stood next to Candace and offered his arm. She placed her hand in the crook of his elbow.

A tear slipped down her cheek, but she quickly dashed it away before anyone else noticed. But he'd seen it. Her eyes met his again. The turmoil in those violet depths made his chest ache and anger blaze in his veins. Lucifer wanted to leap up onto the balcony and pull her hand off the prince's.

Marriage? She is mine. She is not marrying anyone. Did she think I wouldn't find out about this?

The queen was still droning on, but everything else around him faded away. All their focus was on each other. Why had she kept this from him? She'd told him she was his and yet here she was engaged to be married. Was it merely for convenience, to bind their families together? There were too many questions. He would make her answer them all. She was not getting out of any of it. He was going to make sure she knew who she belonged to.

The sound of people clapping around him brought him back into the room. He glanced at the queen who'd finally finished talking. She was staring at Candace. She followed her daughter's line of sight to him. The queen's eyes narrowed. He'd hidden who he really was from everyone bar Candace, but perhaps he should show himself to Gwilliana. Show her that her daughter belonged to him. The urge passed as soon as it came.

No. It is clear she is forcing Candace into this. Causing trouble for her is not what I wish.

Despite his anger at her lies and secrets, he would not antagonise the queen until he had answers.

"Now, our young couple will open our ball with the first dance," Gwilliana said with a flourish.

Theodus led Candace down the stairs to the side of the balcony. The fae dispersed to the sides of the room, leaving them alone in the middle of the floor. She placed one hand in the prince's and the other on his shoulder. The music tinkled through the room and they began to move.

Lucifer clenched his fists. Her luscious curves in that dress drove him crazy.

I want to tear it off her. Have her beneath me again. I need her heat and the way she looks at me with such affection. My little witch.

He'd missed everything about the woman dancing with another man. She'd found a way to dig herself right into his immortal soul. They'd never be free of each other. That much was clear. Her gaze kept falling on him.

He listened, drowning out the other sounds so he could hear their soft conversation with each other.

"It has been a long time, Cadmi," the prince said.

"Yes, I suppose it has."

"Your mother tells me you do not wish to be involved in the wedding preparations."

"Looking at flowers and pretty dresses all day? I think not."

The prince smiled at her, light green eyes twinkling with amusement. Lucifer didn't like the way the prince was looking at Candace.

"No, you were never such a delicate soul unlike those of your mother's court. Your dual nature I suppose."

"My witch blood you mean. Does it repulse you as it does the others?"

"Did your mother not tell you? I put myself forward when she approached the other courts to find you a mate."

He could hardly blame this prince. Candace was beautiful with fire running in her veins. She was from two different worlds and to him, she was everything.

"Why would you do that? Everyone hates me. Well, I suppose now they know who I really am that might change."

Candace looked away from him. Her eyes seeking out Lucifer again. The expression on her face almost made him take a step towards her. There was longing in her eyes.

"Because you and I are not so different."

"I see."

Her gaze was still stuck on him and not the prince. He needed to be patient. Bide his time until he could demand answers from her. He would possess Candace again. Own every inch of her body as she trembled and clenched around him. It would be sweet, delicious torture. Worth each moment they spent joined with each other.

When her dance with the prince came to an end, her hand was claimed by another prominent member of fae society. She danced with many until she was finally alone. She stood by the windows of the ballroom, staring out at the grounds with a faraway look in her eyes.

No one seemed to be paying attention to her. He silently approached her. His hand curled around her lower back. He leant close to her ear.

"Hello again," he whispered.

She shivered turning to him with wide eyes. Her perfect mouth fell open on a gasp. The next moment it snapped shut and her eyes blazed with anger.

"What are you doing here?" she hissed.

"I'm here to see you. Haven't you missed me in your bed?"

"You shouldn't be here. Fuck. Do you have any idea how much shit I'll be in if she finds out about you?"

His fingers brushed over the skin above the scandalously low back of her dress. He felt her lean into his touch.

She can't help it, can she? She craves me as much as I do her. I will have her. I will have her again and she won't be able to deny me. That prince be damned. She is mine and she knows it.

"I am not leaving until you and I have a little talk. Don't you think you owe me that much after you kept the truth of who you are from me?"

Chapter Sixteen

here was silence between them for several moments. She glanced around the room, but it seemed no one was looking their way. Her expression was resigned when she turned back to him.

"Not here. We can't talk here. I'm not supposed to leave. I'm the guest of honour."

"Then dance with me."

He didn't allow her to object. He took her hand and tugged her out onto the floor where the next song was beginning. The heat of her body drove him crazy. He tugged her closer, his hand splayed across her back.

"What are you doing?" she hissed.

"Don't make a scene," he whispered.

She put her hand on his shoulder. Her face was flushed. They started to move to the music, twirling around the other couples.

"We're too close."

Their bodies were pressed together, his fingers dangerously low. There were a few disapproving looks from the fae around them.

"Stop. If she sees you with me like this, she'll know."

"You forget, you are mine, Candace or should I call you Cadmi?"

"Don't do this now, please. I promise I'll explain everything."

He leant closer, his breath fanning across her cheek.

"You are mine."

She was silent, her violet eyes wide with fear and desire.

She can never hide it from me.

There were no further objections from her mouth. He could feel her arousal coursing through her veins. He knew she could feel his pressed up against her stomach. Every movement between them made the ache worse.

When the music came to an end, she took his hand, pulling him away towards one of the doors. She glanced around before tugging him through it, down the hallway and into an empty room. Letting go of his hand when she closed the door, she turned to him. There was nothing but pure unadulterated lust in her expression. No words needed to be spoken.

He slammed her up against the door, their mouths fused together in an electrifying and brutal kiss. Her hands were at his belt, tugging it open before she tugged down the zip of his trousers and freed him. He pulled up her dress, pushing aside her underwear. He stroked his fingers across her softness, feeling her arousal running down her legs. She groaned, tugging his hips towards her.

Fuck, you're always so wet for me. Only for me. I command your body, don't I?

He sunk into her in one swift movement. She wrapped both legs around his back, his hands under her behind, holding her up and pinning her to the door. One of her hands was around his neck, the other holding his face.

He'd missed her touch with a force which threatened to break him. He would give her a piece of his mind later. Now all he wanted was to be inside her. To feel her heat consuming him with every stroke. That dress had been driving him crazy all night.

"Yes, yes you do. I've missed you so much. Everything about you. I need you. Fuck, do I need you, Lucifer."

He pounded into her with all he was worth. She bit down on his bottom lip, whimpering. They both needed to be quiet least someone came along and heard them together.

Tell me you're mine.

She turned away from him, burying her face in his shoulder.

"I'm yours," she whispered.

"Say it again."

"I'm yours, Lucifer."

He growled, thrusting harder. She bit down on his suit jacket.

"Are you going to come all over me, Candace?"

"Yes, yes, fuck. I'm so close."

He wanted to make her snap, to hear her scream, but now wasn't the time. She rested her head back against the door, staring at him with unfocused eyes. He reached up, putting a hand over her mouth. Seconds later she was crying out, the sounds muffled as her body quaked and clenched around him.

Fuck, I can never hold back when she comes. It's too much. She's too much.

He grunted, feeling his own ending pulsating through him. All the tension of the past two weeks away from her eased.

When he removed his hand from her mouth, her head dropped on his shoulder, her breath coming fast. Her fingers curled into the hair at the back of his neck, anchoring him to her.

"I never wanted to leave. All I want is you," she said, her voice quiet.

Her words made his heart ache. There had been no question about what she wanted. She'd made it very clear to him before she left. It didn't change anything.

"We need to talk."

"Not here. Fuck, I shouldn't have even left the room."

She turned her head, looking up at him.

"Mmm, was your need to have me overriding your sense of duty, perhaps?"

"Oh, just... shut up."

She moved, pressing her mouth to his. Her longing poured out of her. He moved in her again. Her fingers dug into his head.

"Stop. Not again. I need to get back."

His need to possess her utterly almost outweighed his common sense. He wanted to fuck her where he could make her scream. Hear her cries of pleasure whilst he ruined her. This was not the place for that. He pulled away, allowing her to drop back down to her feet. Her face was flushed, her breathing still a little laboured. She had that well and truly fucked look about her. It was for him alone. No one else was allowed to see her this way.

He clicked his fingers. Her dress readjusted itself around her, her hair perfectly in place again. His suit was immaculate. No one would know they'd just snuck away for a moment of passionate, mind-bending sex. Candace was the only woman he wanted to fuck and fuck again until she was his completely.

She's mine to ruin. Only mine.

"Just give me half an hour, okay? I'll get away somehow and we can talk," she said, looking down at herself.

"Fine."

She brushed her fingers across his cheek lightly before she slipped from the room. His own fingers traced where hers had been. Her violet eyes had been full of affection.

She told me she cares for me, but is it more than that? Does she feel as I do? Am I everything to her as she is to me? Do I own my little witch's heart?

Why did the thought of that make his pound so hard in his chest?

Candace stood outside the room for a moment, catching her breath.

Lucifer was here.

Here.

How could he be here?

And now he knew.

Knew her secrets.

She'd known she was going to have to marry to unite her distant cousin's family to hers. It wasn't so much she minded Theodus. She'd only met him a handful of times and didn't know him very well.

It hadn't mattered before.

It mattered now.

Now her heart was otherwise engaged.

The thought of submitting to anyone else but Lucifer made her skin crawl.

It would be her duty to provide an heir. She would never be queen, but her child would inherit the crown when Gwilliana passed. The fae thought their queen was barren. She had conceived Candace in secret. Only the royal courts knew of her existence.

I don't want to sleep with Theodus. I don't want him touching me in the places Lucifer has. All I want is the angel behind that door.

She shook herself, striding away back into the ballroom. She could only hope no one had noticed her absence. Now, she just had to work out how to slip away entirely so she could have it out with Lucifer. There was no question it was going to be tumultuous.

A hand darted out and wrapped around her wrist. She was tugged into an alcove. Looking up, she found her betrothed staring down at her.

"Where have you been?" he asked in a low voice.

"I needed a moment. All of this has been very overwhelming." The lie rolled off her tongue with ease.

"I saw you leave with him."

The blood froze in her veins. Theodus couldn't know about Lucifer.

"With who?"

"A fae with dark hair. You and he were dancing rather close to one another."

He wasn't fae. Had Lucifer hidden his identity from everyone but her? It was the only logical explanation.

"Just someone from my past, but they don't matter."

The more lies she told, the worse she felt. This man was to be her husband. And yet, he could never have her in the way the man who haunted her every second could. She was already owned by another. A man who made her molten with desire, drove her crazy with anger, lust, fear and who's gentleness threatened to break her entirely. He'd almost won. If she let him in any further, he would ruin her completely.

"If it doesn't matter then why are you so jittery?"

Fuck. He's seen right through me. I've just been fucked by someone else who I can't afford to love.

She was fucked up for loving the Devil. There was no question about that.

"Can I ask you to do something for me?"

"What?"

"I need to leave. I have unfinished business and it can't wait. I hate to ask this of you, but can you tell her I had too much wine or something, anything?"

He stared at her for the longest time, his expression blank. Hating that she knew very little about the man she was meant to marry, she waited.

He'd said they were alike, but what did that really mean? Was he caged too? Caged by duty?

I was caged by it, but now I'm caged by something entirely different.

Lucifer.

Her heart was caged by him. He owned her body, her heart and her soul.

"Fine, go. Promise me one thing."

"What?"

"You'll come see me tomorrow. We have a lot to discuss about our future."

It wasn't a difficult request.

"Okay. I can do that."

He gave her a soft smile. She slipped from the alcove and disappeared back through the door she'd dragged Lucifer through earlier. He was leaning up against the wall. Dark, mesmerising eyes glinting with barely controlled anger and frustration.

She took his hand, feeling the tension radiating off his skin. It made her flinch. There was none of the affection, lust, desire from before. Only the dark angel she'd come to fear yet who's brutality made her blood pound in her ears with uncontrolled need remained.

"Come," she said.

They walked down the long hallway together. She opened a door at the end. It was a dark room, but the moonlight shone through the large patio doors.

Opening one, they slipped out into the night.

"Where do you live?" he asked.

"Hasn't Mall been feeding you information about me?"

His dark eyes flashed. He'd found out she was going to be here because of his assistant. She cursed Mall in her head for being so loyal to her lord and master. As much as she liked the succubus, Mall still answered to the angel in front of her.

"Do not test my patience."

She told him, not wanting the punishment he'd dish out if she refused. Large white wings unfurled from his back and a halo of golden light appeared above his head. Her mouth fell open. Heat pooled between her thighs at the sight of him.

Holy fuck. I thought he was stunning before, but shit, this is who he truly is behind all that darkness.

A perfect angel.

His hand snapped over her wrist, pulling her to him.

"Hold on, my little witch," he said.

The term of endearment sent her pulse into overdrive. He'd never called her anything but Candace or girl before.

His little witch. Why does that make me love him all the more?

He picked her up. Her arms curled around his neck. White wings flared out before they beat once, twice and then they shot into the sky.

"How come you never showed me this before?" she called over the rushing sound of the wind.

"The Devil cannot show himself in his true form in Hell. It would ruin his image."

"Why me then? You didn't need to show me all of it."

His mouth was close to her ear, breath tickling her neck.

"It made you ache for me, didn't it? The longing in your eyes would've been enough, but I feel your desire pulsating in you like wildfire. Don't you understand by now? I want to see you burn for me whilst I ruin every inch of you. You. Are. Mine."

Potent lust punctuated every word he spoke. The possessiveness of his tone made her core ache and pulsate. The wild, passionate fuck against the door was nothing compared to what she knew he was capable of. He'd not given her all his brutality yet. A part of her wondered if she could take it. If Lucifer well and truly ruined her, could she ever perform her duty to her family? Could she marry Theodus and provide her mother with an heir?

The darkness in his eyes glittered in the moonlight. It sent a tingle down her spine and she trembled.

What will he do to me when we get to my place? Will it involve punishment for keeping the truth from him?

Chapter Seventeen

*a*fter they'd landed and she'd let him into her flat, he stood near the door, eying her open plan living area with an inscrutable gaze. She kicked off her high heels and walked over to the window, staring out into the gloom.

"Explain."

That one word stabbed at her heart. His tone was deadly, broking no objections. This was the moment she never wanted to come. The one where she told the man she loved why she had to perform her duty which was now abhorrent to her.

"My father had an affair with her which spanned five years until she fell pregnant with me. They kept it hidden from all but the royal courts. I was only two days old when she gave me to my father in exchange for a promise that when I turned twenty-five, I would return to the fae as their princess. She thinks I'm their saviour because of that ridiculous prophecy, but no one even understands it or knows whether it is really related to the fae."

Taking a moment to gather her thoughts, she turned to him. His eyes betrayed nothing.

"My father never lied to me about my duty. I'm under no illusions about what's expected of me. She wants me to provide her with an heir. That is my purpose to her, nothing more."

And I was okay with it until I met you. Until I fell in love with you.

Those were the words she couldn't say.

"That's it?" he asked.

"What else can I say? I've waited my entire life for this day. I've known for five years who she'd chosen for me. I'd accepted it, but now, it's all fucked up because you're here and in my life. Don't you see I had to leave for my own sake?"

He advanced on her with slow, calculated steps. His hand shot out, curling around her arm in an almost painful grip.

"Do you not want me here?"

"Of course, I fucking do. Haven't I made that clear? All I want is you but I can't have you. I'm yours, but you are not mine. None of this is mine. I have to do what I was born to do."

His eyes darkened, his expression turning feral. It should've scared the living daylights out of her, but she wasn't scared by his darkness any longer. A part of her craved it, wanted him to be ruthless with her.

"Do you want that prince to fuck you? Use you as his broodmare for your mother's sake?"

What the fuck? Does he think I actually want to be fucked by someone else other than him? Is he insane?

Whatever hold she had on her temper shattered. She was done with accusations.

"As if you wouldn't fucking do the same. Use me until you get bored then toss me aside like I mean nothing to you."

His grip tightened causing her to yelp. The look in his eyes made her heart ache. There was rage, fury but there was also a tiny flicker of pain. Like her words actually hurt him.

"Let go!"

"Is that what you really think of me? Do you think I care nothing for you? Do you?"

"How the fuck should I know how you feel about me? I don't even know why the hell you're here, tormenting me with things I can't possibly have."

Wanting to slam all of her words back in her mouth, she glared at him. Why did he have to make her so angry? Why did he have to say such provoking things? She hated it. All of it. Most of all she hated herself for being too weak to push him away. To tell him to leave and never come back because she wasn't strong enough to walk away.

Her heart bled for him. Behind the façade she saw the tortured angel who'd been twisted by ruling over Hell. All she wanted was to be his solace. The person he needed because she needed him like he was the very air she breathed. But that angel was hidden from her now. In his place stood the Devil. The man who'd take everything from her. Who'd ruin her with his brutality and flay her heart alive with his cruel words.

"If that's the man you think I am, then that's the man you'll get, my little witch."

That term of endearment shattered everything inside her. It was said with malice, not affection. He dragged her over to the dining room table, shoving her onto it. Her stomach connected with the edge, winding her. He folded himself over her, flattening her palms on the wood.

"I told you that first day, you shouldn't play games with the Devil. You'll only get burnt."

His breath tickled her ear. Her pulse pounded erratically. He was entirely unpredictable in his moods.

"Lucifer, this isn't funny."

He moved off her, but when she tried to move, she found her hands stuck like glue.

Does he think this is okay with me?

"What the fuck? Stop this, let me go."

He said nothing, trailing his fingers down her back. He gripped her thighs, spreading her legs wide. Her feet got stuck to the floor. She was rendered utterly immobile by his power. A cold sweat beaded at the back of her neck. Never before had she been so vulnerable in front of another person.

"Don't do this, please, Lucifer, please. I don't want this."

His laugh was haunted.

"My little witch. You said you want me, but you don't even understand what that really means. I won't hold back any more. You've asked for the Devil and he is who you're getting."

Her limbs shook. The dangerous note in his voice flooded her with heat.

Why the fuck am I getting turned on by him right now? I'm so fucked up. I don't even want to be in this position.

"Stop."

His fingers trailed up her inner thighs. A small growl left his lips when he found her wet and wanting, fingers brushing over her sex through her underwear.

"Your mouth lies, but this does not. You like this. You want me to punish you."

"No, I don't."

She struggled against her invisible bonds. This was the second time he'd restrained her, but last time she'd wanted it. Now she was half terrified of what he'd do next.

She heard him click his fingers. She felt the wood on her bare skin, grazing against her nipples. He'd done it again. Stripped her without a second thought.

Pain radiated up her behind when his palm came down, hard.

"Do you think I wanted to watch you with other men? Your body pressed against them whilst you danced?"

Another smack. She flinched, whimpering. His hands weren't gentle.

This is his punishment. Fuck. He's going to hurt me because I left him.

"The thought of that prince with his paws on your skin fills me with uncontrollable rage, my little witch. You are not his to touch. Your body doesn't belong to him nor does any other part of you."

No. I belong to you. I love you, Lucifer, even if I hate you for what you're doing to me right now.

Four more strikes, each one harder than the next. Her entire behind radiated with heat and pain.

"Mmm, your skin is blossoming red, but it's not enough. I want more. I want to brand myself on you. I want everyone to know you're mine."

She lost count of the times he hit her. All she could hear was the sound of his palm smacking against her skin and his exhale with each strike.

"Please, stop, it hurts," she whispered.

What she didn't say was her entire body felt tight, needing a release from the pain, from the pulsating in her core. Her arousal trickled down her inner thighs.

"You can beg me, Candace. Beg me to stop, but I know you want this. I can feel it."

As if to prove it, his fingers ran up the seam of her sex. She whimpered in response, wanting him to fuck her with them. Desperately needing him to give her something more. She wriggled, trying to gain purchase, to encourage him.

"Tell me what you want," he said, his voice seductive and low.

"You. I want you."

There was no room left for lies.

"Do you want Lucifer or the Devil?"

"Both. I want both. Fuck. I want all of you. Every part. You have no idea how much I burn for you. Every night I dream of you and wake up hot and wet with need."

"Do you want that prince? Do you crave his skin against yours?"

She whimpered when he smacked her again.

"No. Shit. Lucifer, no. My body is yours. My fucking everything is yours. Take it all. I'm giving you everything. Just please stop torturing me like this."

His fingers danced down her back, trailing circles across her skin. She arched up against him as much as she could with her limbs stuck to the table and the floor.

"Come back to Hell with me."

His demand made her heart crack. It was already shattered, but he was breaking it further.

How is it even possible for my heart to take this much pain?

"You know I can't do that."

"Can't or won't?"

Another smack came. This one stung like nothing else. She cried out, tears pricking at the corners of her eyes.

"Please, I told you why. It's my duty. Don't you understand? I thought this was my prison sentence, but I didn't know anything. Not until you turned up and placed me in your gilded cage. I'm not free. She put me in chains, but you... you've caged me. And fuck... you're ruining everything just like you wanted. You've ruined me for everyone else."

It was like something snapped between them. One minute his hand was resting on her behind, the next he pressed up against her entrance and slammed into her up to the hilt in one thrust. His fingers dug into her hips, pounding into her with absolutely no mercy. It hurt, but it felt incredible all the same.

Holy fucking hell.

He leant over her, his breath harsh against her face.

"Have I really broken you, my little witch?"

"Yes," she whimpered.

His skin pressed against her heated behind burnt and stung, each thrust dragging his flesh against hers.

"Mmm, I don't think I have. You're still denying me. You're still going to marry that boy. He won't make you happy. He won't fuck you like you need. Punish you when you disobey him. He'll use you until you've given your mother what she desires. He won't care for you. You need me. Need me to fuck you and care for you afterwards like you're the most precious person in the world. Because that's what you are to me, my little witch. Precious. You still think I don't care for you? Haven't I shown you how much I want you? I left Hell to retrieve you. To bring you home."

The weight of his words threatened to suffocate her.

He cares about me? How the fuck did this happen? I want to give in. I want to go home with him. I belong to him.

Tears fell down, darkening the wood below her. He thrust harder. The table dug into her hips, but she didn't care any longer. All she could feel was Lucifer, his heart racing against her back, his power washing over her, inching her towards an earth-shattering orgasm. His fingers curled over hers.

"Tell me you're mine," he whispered, his voice soft.

"I'm yours."

"Do you want to know a secret?"

She nodded, unable to speak any longer.

"I wasn't lying when I told you I've never held a woman in the way I hold you. I've never wanted a woman in the way I want you. I crave your skin against mine. I crave every part of you. I want to hear your voice even when you say such cruel words. Tell me you hate me when I know it's the opposite. My little witch, you've ensnared me with all that you are."

I'm ruined. Utterly ruined. Lucifer, I love you. Every inch of you. You're cruel and brutal, but you're everything I need because you care for me too.

"But there's more, Candace... It was Mall who told me to be gentle with you. She told me you were fragile inside and that if I wanted you to come willingly, I should show you I could be gentle."

Mall. The succubus had seen right through her. How did Mall know that? How did she see that they needed each other? Lucifer had etched himself on her heart.

"Why did you listen to her?"

"I never wanted to force you. I wanted you to be mine because you wanted it that way."

Tears fell harder. His hands gripped hers, a groan escaping his mouth as he pressed deeper. Sparks ran up her spine, warning her she was on the edge. Once, twice more he thrust into her and the dam broke. She cried out, shuddering and trembling beneath him.

"That's right. Scream my name, my little witch."

She didn't hold back, crying out as wave after wave of pure bliss consumed her whole.

"Fuck, Lucifer."

He grunted, pulsating inside her. She could feel every inch of him and it only drove her higher. Even though her behind still smarted from his brutal spanking, she floated in the clouds.

How is it that he does this to me? How can he take command of my body, know what I want before I do?

He didn't disengage from her immediately. His breathing was heavy, his body almost crushing hers.

"I want to mark you. So you know you're mine. So everyone knows I have claimed you as my own."

Chapter Eighteen

Candace blinked, turning her face to look up at him. His dark eyes glittered with emotions she didn't understand.

"What do you mean?" she asked.

"Mmm, I'm going to give you the mark of the Devil."

She froze underneath him. *What the actual fuck?* Did he really think he could just do that without her objecting to it?

"No. I already know I'm yours. You can't do that."

"I wasn't asking for your permission."

Anger flooded her immediately. He pulled off her, running his hands over her behind. She flinched away from his fingers. A tingling sensation ran down her skin, the sting of his spanking faded. He'd healed her just like he had done when he'd brutally pounded her mouth, leaving her jaw aching.

"I will hurt you again then I'll care for you, my little witch."

"What the fuck, Lucifer? You can't just tell me you're going to give me the mark of the Devil then start on about how you want to hurt me. And what the fuck is with you calling me your little witch? Where did that come from?"

His breath fluttered over her thighs. She hadn't realised he'd knelt down behind her.

"Mmm, where should I brand you? You're mine and a witch, are you not?"

Not knowing how to respond to either of those questions, she kept her mouth shut.

Is that how he's thought of me all along? As his? His witch?

His fingers trailed down her calves. He gripped her ankle, pulling her foot from the floor and placing it in his lap. His fingers brushed over the sensitive arch. She shuddered.

"I think I'm going to place it here." His fingertips traced a line around her right ankle, just above the bone. "It'll be fitting. Don't worry, it will only hurt for a moment."

She didn't get a chance to open her mouth when the pain shot up her leg. She whimpered, tears falling again. It burnt. Every touch of his finger against her skin until he was done.

He'd branded her.

Marked her as his.

She was broken.

He'd ruined everything.

How could she hide this? Her mother would never see it, but Theodus would. The man who would be her husband would see she was owned by someone else. Someone brutal. Someone who showed her no mercy. But someone she loved with a fierceness which consumed her whole.

"Fuck you," she whispered.

He ran his fingers over the mark she couldn't see.

"It's beautiful, just like you, Candace, little witch. You're mine."

He placed her foot back down on the floor, his touch caressing rather than possessive.

"I'm going to take care of you now."

The hold he had over her released. Her limbs trembled. She wasn't sure she could stand on her own after what he'd done to her. She was angry at him for branding her, but the fight inside her died. All she wanted was for him to hold her and never let go. The fucked up part of her loved him for everything he'd done and everything he'd promised to do.

He picked her up off the table, cradling her to his chest.

"Where is your bathroom?" he asked, his voice soft.

"The first door next to the kitchen. The second door is my bedroom."

He carried her into the bathroom, setting her down on the edge of the bath. Her skin was damp with sweat and her arousal had run down her legs. He reached into her shower and flipped it on. Taking her hands, he helped her stand up and brought her under the water. He ran his hands over her hair which untangled her braids.

"Lucifer..." she whispered.

"Shh, we can talk when you're clean."

It didn't seem right to object to that. She let him wash her, soaping her body with her coconut shower gel. His fingers were gentle. The man before her was Lucifer and not the Devil. He was the damaged angel who was taking care of her. His little witch.

When he was satisfied she was clean, he bundled her up in a towel. His power brushed over her, drying her hair and skin.

He led her into her bedroom, pulling back the covers and tugging her down into the bed with him. She wrapped her arms around his back, pressing her face into his chest.

Why does he feel so much like home? Am I crazy for loving this man? This angel who punished me and fucked me and confessed secrets to me.

"Don't you want to see how I marked you?" he asked.

She did. The curiosity burnt inside her, but what could she even say? He wouldn't take it away if she hated it. She shook her head. It was a problem she could deal with tomorrow. Just like all her other problems. She'd promised to see Theodus and talk about their future. The one she didn't want and had no real say in.

"You're going to leave when I fall asleep, aren't you?"

"Everything has been unsettled since the portals reopened."

"Then we really broke whatever God did to prevent anyone from leaving? The three of us did?"

"Yes. I have had to stop all my dukes from disappearing. Chaos will reign if I do not keep them in line."

She clutched him closer. Tension radiated from him. She ran a hand down his back, trying to soothe it away. Her fingers trailed, brushing over his skin. He murmured his approval.

"I've missed your touch," he whispered.

"You have?"

"Mmm, your soft skin soothes me. Do you really dream of me and wake up in torment?"

"Why would I say it if I didn't? I cried myself to sleep the night I left you. I argued with my father the next day and got horribly drunk on whisky with a friend. I felt like shit, but I woke up burning with need to feel you against me despite the hangover."

His arms around her tightened.

"A friend? Not Jaxon?"

She flinched at her best friend's name. There had been no time for her to talk things out with him or maybe she just didn't want to make time. She wasn't sure how she felt telling Lucifer about Alistair but lying to him had only led to punishment.

"Jax and I aren't exactly talking because he wants to know what happened between us. So, no, it was another friend."

Something Alistair said tickled at her memory.

"He told me about the Darkness. He was there."

Lucifer went deadly still. She pulled away, staring up into his face, which was haunted.

"Will you tell me about it now?"

His expression shut down, his eyes blazing with something she didn't understand.

"What is there to say? I tried to prevent it all, but Azrael was so obsessed with that girl. She was sent to destroy the world, you know. The vessel. I suppose it was resolved in the end. It was all part of His plan to punish Azrael because I apparently poisoned His children against Him. I did nothing but tell them they deserved the same freedom He granted humanity. Now Azrael lives happily up in Heaven with her and the rest of my brothers and sisters whilst I am consigned to spend eternity in servitude to Hell."

Every word made her heart contract further.

All that pain inside him. All that resentment. I want to dig it out and lay bare his wounds so I can heal them all. And if he wants to take out his suffering on me, then so be it. I want to be his everything because he is mine.

Knowing what she wanted and knowing she could never have those things sliced into her like a knife. Tearing her insides to shreds. And she couldn't prevent the tears from slipping down her face.

"What is it?" he asked, his face suddenly concerned.

"Do you know how much I want you? Not just the things you choose to show me, but all of you, even the tormented and damaged parts you keep hidden away? And how much it breaks me knowing none of it is mine?"

His eyes betrayed so much. Shock. Confusion. Affection. Longing. All of it flittering across his expression in quick succession.

"Am I everything to you?" he whispered.

"Yes. Everything and more."

She was done with keeping the truth of her feelings from him.

"Then come home with me, my little witch. I'll take you away from your fate."

"I can't."

As much as she desperately wanted to, she didn't belong with him in Hell. She didn't deserve him nor his gentleness or his torment. Not when she was supposed to be marrying someone else. He shouldn't be in her bed, but she didn't care. If she could have these moments with Lucifer whilst everything else burnt around her, then she would.

He leant towards her, capturing her mouth in a soft kiss. Hands stroked circles along her back, fingers trailed along her sides. She felt him everywhere, caressing her. In that moment, she knew he was Lucifer, not the Devil. And he was going to make love to her rather than fuck her. Blood pounded in her ears. This was everything she needed. No more words were uttered.

She drowned in him.

And he ruined her with every heartfelt kiss he pressed to her skin.

Lucifer watched her sleeping for the longest time. He finally understood all the emotions coursing through him. Finally made sense of what she meant to him.

I love her.

It wasn't something he thought he was capable of, but he loved Candace with every beat of his heart, every breath he took.

My little witch has stolen my heart and made it her own.

He knew he needed to return to Hell, but he couldn't tear himself away from her. She'd accepted his darker side with no question despite her vocal objections to his punishment. Seeing her so vulnerable and open made him want to hurt her even more. It was sick and twisted, but her cries of pleasure and pain fed him in a way no one else had.

He'd treated other women in this way, but he'd never been driven to soothe them afterwards. To punish and adore, worship every inch of their body. He wanted to spend the rest of eternity doing so to her. Candace would live longer than a regular human. She was half fae and they lived centuries.

He shook himself. Now was not the time to be thinking about these things. There were so many pressing matters awaiting him. If she was refusing to come back with him, he wouldn't force her, yet.

Under no circumstances was she marrying that fae prince. He'd make her see she couldn't.

Her foot was sticking out from under the covers. The mark he'd left on her stark against her skin.

No one will be able to take her from me now.

Slipping out of bed, he ran a hand through her blonde hair, stroking it away from her face. He pressed a kiss to her forehead.

"I'll be back for you."

The next minute he was outside and airborne, soaring over London until he landed in the place he'd left Hell by. Stepping into the portal, he arrived back in the throne room within minutes. Mall was pacing, her expression wary. She inclined her head when he strolled in.

"My Lord," she said.

She looked behind him, as if expecting someone else. Her face fell when she realised he was alone.

"Where is Candace? I thought you went to retrieve her."

He sat on his throne, drumming his fingers on the arm.

"She's at home on Earth."

Mall strode over to him. Her eyes were wide with fear.

"Lucifer, you should've brought her back. She's not safe."

She never called him by his name. His eyes snapped to hers, a frown appearing across his brow.

"Explain."

"Dantalion and Beleth have gone to Earth to find her. I fear they mean to torture her or worse. I thought she was safe because she was with you, but now..."

Blood pounded in his ears at her words.

"Why did you not prevent them from leaving?"

"I only heard after they were gone. I apologise, my Lord."

She bowed her head, shame in her eyes. He rose from his throne. Rage. All he could feel was rage.

If they've laid a hand on her, I will tear them in half.

He could not blame Mall for their actions, but she was meant to keep an eye on things for him. He'd left her in charge.

"Stay here and make sure no other fuck ups happen in my absence. Can you do that?"

Her head was still bowed. He didn't have time to deal with her.

"Yes, of course, my Lord."

"Good. Now, excuse me, I have two demons to slaughter."

And with that, he strode from the room.

Chapter Nineteen

he ground shook as he landed in the street outside Candace's flat. His wings flared out of his back, looking every part the dark, fallen angel that he was.

The two demons in their human forms had a hold of a girl between them, her blonde hair covering her face. Beleth and Dantalion stopped dead when they saw him.

"Fuck," muttered Beleth.

The girl looked up. Her lip was split, a dark bruise forming around her left eye, which was swollen shut. Violent rage simmered inside him, threatening to burst out at any moment. They'd hurt her.

Her mouth fell open, but no sound came out. There were dark bruises around her throat. She was only wearing the t-shirt he'd put on her before he left, but it was torn in places, exposing her skin to the air.

How could they have done this in the time I was gone? I'm going to kill them. They've gone too far this time.

"I am going to give you five seconds to release her and kneel at my feet," he said with barely contained fury in his voice.

It took one second for Dantalion to drop Candace's arm and rush towards him, pressing his knees to the ground, head bowed. She swayed on her feet, falling into Beleth's side. The demon stood there, staring at Lucifer with a challenge in his eyes.

"I'm sorry, my Lord. It was him. He made me come. I didn't touch her," Dantalion said, his words frantic.

Lucifer ignored him. He didn't care what the demon had to say for himself. It was obvious Beleth had instigated this.

My little witch has suffered too much.

His eyes fell to her bare legs where there were scratches and welts.

"Stay there, Dantalion, do not move an inch," he said.

He stepped around the demon, taking several steps towards Beleth and Candace.

"Don't come any closer," Beleth said, wrapping his hand around Candace's neck. "I will kill her if you do."

"Tell me, what do you hope to gain from this?"

There had been chaos in Hell since the portals reopened, but this was something else. There was no reason for his dukes to be restless any longer. They were free, but perhaps this freedom had come at a price. He needed to teach them a lesson. Put them back in their place.

"You are no real leader, Lucifer. No one fears Hell any more. You are weak. Gone soft. She is proof of it. You say she's your toy, but I don't believe that for a second. Why would you allow her to leave and go back to her life otherwise? So, I'm taking her."

Did Beleth truly believe he'd gone soft? The demon was about to get a wake-up call. Beleth had hurt the woman he loved. It broke something inside him seeing her battered and bruised by someone other than him. She was his to ruin.

"Weak? You think me weak?" He laughed, the sound echoing around the street. "Oh, Beleth, you really have no idea what you've awoken."

A huge, long black whip appeared in his hand. He cracked it. The sound made Candace flinch back. Beleth's fingers were still around her neck.

"I'll tell you one last time, release her."

Beleth's eyes blazed with anger.

"No."

Lucifer's eyes began to glow red, his entire persona changed from light to darkness. His wings turned black, a halo of fire appearing atop his head. Black armour built itself around his chest, arms and legs, glinting in the moonlight. The dark angel he truly was sprung free. The Devil who had no restraints. There was nothing holding him back any longer and Beleth would feel the full brunt of his wrath.

Candace's good eye widened slightly. Her expression wasn't one of fear, but complete awe. If he had any doubts about how she felt for him, he didn't any longer. She'd once told him he wasn't a knight in shining armour, but now, that's very much what he was. Her fucked up knight and he would rescue her from everything as long as the two of them continued to breathe.

He brought the whip up and it cracked again.

"Do you still wish to disobey me, Beleth?" he said, his voice not quite sounding like his own.

The demon glared at him.

"I see. Well, I'm going to send you back where you belong."

The whip sprung forward, wrapping around Beleth's neck. Once. Twice. Three times. He pulled it taut. The demon didn't release Candace, but his eyes began to bulge in their sockets. It was time he paid for hurting Lucifer's woman.

"You're nothing, Lucifer," Beleth said, his voice higher than usual and breathy. "Even your own father cast you out. No one cares about the Devil any longer."

Lucifer pulled the whip tighter, cutting off the demon's airway. Beleth released Candace's arm, putting his hand to the whip, trying to prevent it from strangling him. His fingers tightened on Candace's neck. She whimpered slightly. Lucifer took a step towards them, pulling the whip ever tighter.

"You think your words cut me, Beleth. It is you who is nothing. Worthless. Your daughter hates you. You thought you could use her, but she is more than you'll ever be. She is my kin too, you know. You've forgotten who your master is. I was made by the Divine. I hold His power in the palm of my hands. I can end you with a click of my fingers."

He wasn't going to kill Beleth. There were far worse things than death and his demon would suffer them all. He'd make sure of it.

"I will see you in Hell."

His grip on the whip tightened as he pulled. It dug into Beleth's neck, slicing through flesh. The demon flailed, dropping Candace who collapsed onto her knees, unable to hold herself up. Both Beleth's hands went to his neck as he fell to his knees too. He stared up at Lucifer, his eyes wide with hatred but also fear.

A final tug sawed through bone, disconnecting his head from his body. It dropped to the floor. Black blood sprayed out of his neck coating both Candace and Lucifer. Then his body keeled over and fell to the floor.

Lucifer may have killed his mortal form on Earth, but Beleth would return to Hell. And there, he would be punished.

He turned, finding Dantalion still on his knees, his head bowed.

"Return to Hell if you know what's good for you."

The demon scrambled to his feet, looking up at his lord with fear. His eyes fell on Beleth's decapitated body and he blanched.

"Of course, my Lord. Sorry, my Lord."

Dantalion ran down the street, not looking back.

Lucifer closed the distance between himself and Candace, dropping to his knees. He tucked his fingers under her chin. She stared at him, tears streaming down her face. She looked so broken and it tore at his soul.

"I'm sorry," he whispered. "I'm sorry I left and they did this to you."

She reached out a shaky hand, cupping his cheek. Her thumb traced a line along his bottom lip. She tugged him towards her. Her lips met his with the gentlest of touches.

"I can't talk. He strangled me when I refused to go with them. They waited until you left before they came in and woke me up. They put a cuff on my wrist. It prevented me from using my magic. They wanted to torture me. Both of them. Don't believe the other one, he was just as bad."

He'd known Dantalion was lying to him but chose to allow the demon to think he had gotten away with it. He would suffer just as much as Beleth for their transgressions against Candace.

He pulled away from her, cupping her face. He'd heal every last one of her bruises. His power washed over her, soothing away all of her pain and cleaning away Beleth's black blood. She blinked rapidly, both eyes open. The cuff fell to the ground, he scooped it up.

"Thank you," she whispered. "Thank you for saving me."

She practically threw herself into his arms, clutching him tightly, quiet sobs emitting from her lips. Her fingers trailed over his wings, sending shivers down his spine.

"I'll always protect you, my little witch. You're mine to hurt and ruin, not theirs."

"Yours. I'll always be yours."

He picked her up, cradling her to his chest. She didn't seem to mind his armour. Her head rested on his shoulder, her fingers tracing lines along the curve of his wing.

"That's very distracting."

"Where are we going?"

"You're not safe here. I'm going to take you home. You need to sleep, but I'll return you in the morning. I promise."

He took to the skies without waiting for her response. They soared across London, the lights twinkling below.

"You know, you're stunning even when you're all dark like this. It's like there's two sides of you and only I get to see both of them," she said.

"You're not scared of it?"

"No. I want to see everything. I thought perhaps when you ruined me I might never recover from it, but you see, even when you punish me and hurt me, you still care for me. You aren't disappointed in me like my father. You don't want to use me like my mother. You just want me to be yours because I mean everything to you. I see that now."

He landed in a clearing in Hyde Park. He clicked his fingers and the portal which he'd left by appeared. He carried her through it, back to Hell. When they arrived, he took her straight into his bedroom and gently placed her down on the bed, under the covers. He pressed a kiss to her forehead.

"Sleep. I need to take care of some things," he said.

She put a hand on his arm.

"Lucifer, I... I know what you're going to do, but please come back and hold me afterwards, even if I'm asleep."

The look in her violet eyes made him want to promise her the world. He wanted to get down on his hands and knees and beg her to stay here with him. Beg her for her love and affection.

The past two weeks had proven he couldn't be without her. All he wanted was to drown himself in her citrus and violet scent, in her body. Claim her heart. Her soul.

It was only now he understood the pull Azrael had felt towards Alice. The need to possess and consume her with every moment. He didn't regret what he'd said, but a part of him wished he'd known then how a single person could affect him in this way.

"I will, my little witch."

She smiled at him, letting her hand fall.

That fucking beautiful smile. I want her to only smile like that for me. No one else.

He tucked her hand back in the covers, brushing his fingers over her hair. She looked at him with complete trust. He wanted to be worthy of her even though he knew he wasn't. All the things he wanted to say to her threatened to spill out.

I love you, Candace. I'll give you everything. You are etched on my soul. You have my heart. I can't live in a world where you don't exist.

She closed her eyes, long eyelashes fluttering over her cheeks. It broke the spell between them and he turned away, striding out of the room. Mall was startled when he threw open the doors to the throne room.

"My Lord."

He threw the cuff they'd slapped on Candace at her. She caught it, frowning.

"Return that to Finn. Are they in the pit?" he asked.

"Yes. Is... is she okay?"

Her eyes betrayed her worry for Candace. He hadn't quite realised how much the succubus liked her. Cared for her.

"Yes. She's asleep. Don't go disturbing her. You can see her when she wakes up."

Mall bowed her head.

"Of course."

He nodded at her before striding out into the hallway beyond. The next instant, he was in the pit. Demons who stepped out of line were sent here. He wanted to see to Beleth and Dantalion's punishment himself. The two demons were sitting on a bench, both their hands in chains.

"My Lord," Turnor said, bowing to him.

Turnor ruled the pit with an iron fist. Lucifer didn't often come down here. He wasn't one for watching punishments such as this. This was different. They had hurt Candace. It was time they both learnt their place.

"String them both up," Lucifer said, pointing at Beleth and Dantalion.

"Of course, my Lord," Turnor replied, clicking his fingers at two of his jailors.

They strode forward and dragged Beleth and Dantalion up, tying them both to posts in the corner. Lucifer wandered over to a table. Various implements were draped across it. He picked up a long cat o'nine tails with sharpened silver tips. There were several similar whips. He indicated to Turnor which ones he wanted brought over. The demon signalled the jailors again.

Lucifer walked over to Dantalion with slow, measured steps. Lashing out at the demon's back, the whip left several raised marks on his skin. Dantalion cried out as Lucifer continued to whip him until his back was bloody.

"Continue with this one," he said to Turnor.

He next selected a long, silver tipped whip and moved over to Beleth.

"Now, how many lashes should I give you? How many do you think is fitting for your transgressions? It is not just that you hurt her, Beleth. For the longest time you've tried to punch well above your weight."

The whip cracked. A long red mark appeared on the demon's back. Beleth grunted.

"Trying to overthrow the king. Was that some kind of joke?"

Another crack and two more marks appeared.

"You see, I'm not going to stop until your back is a bloody mess and you're screaming. Then Turnor is going to take over and you'll never see the light of day again. Not only are you stripped of your titles, you are consigned to spend the rest of eternity in servitude to Turnor and his jailors. How does that sound?"

Beleth didn't speak. Lucifer struck again and again. All of his pent-up rage echoed by the crack of the whip and the blood running down Beleth's back. He thought of all the bruises on Candace's skin with each strike. The pain in her eyes. He would never let anyone touch her again.

Crack.

Never again would she be subjected to a demon.

Grunt. Crack.

He'd protect her.

Crack.

He'd save her from her fate.

Crack. Grunt.

Nothing would keep her from him.

Beleth howled under the strain of the pain radiating from his back. Lucifer smiled.

You deserve every last one of these lashes. Each and every one.

The demon slumped on the post, his back ruined beyond repair. Lucifer handed Turnor the whip.

"Don't show him any mercy and make sure they're displayed to the others as a warning to anyone else who wishes to step out of line."

"My Lord," Turnor said, bowing.

Lucifer strode away, listening to the howls of pain from Dantalion and Beleth echoing around the room until the door slammed shut behind him. He'd shown them exactly who he was. The King of Hell. No one would take his place. Even if he hated his father for sending him here, he relished his position all the same.

When he entered his bedroom, Candace was fast asleep, her blonde hair spread out across the pillows.

Fuck, she is so beautiful.

He clicked his fingers, his armour disappeared and was replaced by a t-shirt and boxers. He crawled under the covers next to her. He'd keep his promise. His hand curled around her stomach, pulling her back flush with his front. She stirred a little.

"Is it done?" she whispered, groggily.

"Yes, I'm sorry I woke you."

She turned in his embrace, staring up at him with hazy violet eyes. She cupped his cheek.

"Lucifer... I love you."

She buried her face in his chest, her arm curled around his back. Her breathing dipped into a slow, steady rhythm. He stared down at her, his heart thudding like a drum in his chest.

She... loves me?

Chapter Twenty

Candace paced her living room, wanting to tear her hair out.
Why the fuck did I tell him that? I'm an idiot.

She'd been out of it when he woke her up after he'd punished Beleth and that other demon. He'd saved her, proving he cared more than she realised. And then she'd gone and told him she loved him. It being the truth didn't matter. She shouldn't have said it.

When she'd woken up, he'd still been there, holding her close. He kissed the top of her forehead, murmuring good morning. She'd rolled away to get up, but he'd pulled her against his chest, her back flush with it, his hand splayed out across her stomach.

"Don't go," he whispered in her ear. "Stay with me a little while longer."

Not knowing what to say, she lay there stiffly, unable to speak. The memory of telling him she loved him clashed with her overriding urge to run away because he hadn't said anything about it.

"You're not in any pain, are you?" he asked.

"No, you healed me so I'm okay."

"Mmm, then let me help you relax. You're all tense."

His fingers trailed down her bare arm, the soft touch turning her limbs to jelly.

Damn him. I feel so stupid and yet he's acting like nothing happened. But it did.

She couldn't unsay it. She felt too vulnerable. His distracting touch made it worse. He pressed kisses to her neck and shoulder. And she was lost. They tugged at each other's clothes. It was gentle and unhurried. Him coaxing her into an earth-shattering orgasm as she trembled and bucked against him.

The more time they spent together, the deeper and harder she fell. And now he knew.

She shot out of the bed not long after they were finished, needing distance between them.

"I need to get back. I promised I'd see him today to talk about stuff."

Lucifer hadn't been remotely happy with her pronouncement, but he'd begrudgingly taken her back to her flat after she'd had a brief chat with Mall.

I'm certifiable. I told a man I love him whilst engaged to another. No, not a fucking man. An angel. The original fallen angel.

Her heart felt tight. Could she forsake her entire life, her duty for him? Deep down, she knew the answer to that question and it terrified her.

Her phone buzzed on the kitchen counter. She scooped it up.

"Hello Dad," she said.

"Candace, where are you?"

"Why?"

"Your mother said you left the ball early."

She slapped a hand over her head. Despite asking Theodus to cover for her, she should've known Gwilliana wouldn't let it rest so easily.

"I didn't feel well and I had to deal with something."

"She's here. She expected you to stay with me."

"I promised to see Theodus today. I don't have time for this."

"Candace."

She didn't want to see or speak to her mother.

"Fine, come get me. We wouldn't want to keep the queen waiting."

She heard him sigh.

"You know, she only has your best interests at heart."

"Seriously, Dad? She doesn't care what I want. If she did, she wouldn't be forcing me to marry someone I don't want. She doesn't know anything about me or my life. My wants. My needs."

A purple shimmering light appeared in her living room and her father stepped through. Her mother followed behind him.

"Then why don't you tell her that yourself," Gallian said.

She put the phone down on the counter.

"Thanks for the ambush, Dad," she muttered under her breath.

"Cadmi," her mother said.

"My name is Candace. It has always been regardless of what you named me."

Her father gave her a sharp look. She no longer cared to be civil and polite. The events of last night had left her emotions in a mess. She didn't want to deal with her parents.

"Candace, please explain why you left the ball with a man who was not Theodus."

I should've known someone would tell her about that.

"Why would that be any of your business? I've done everything you asked of me."

"Did you think how it would look to the court?"

Nothing would make her happier than to piss off the fae court. They'd never shown her any respect or courtesy until they discovered she was their princess. It was all so false.

"Do you think I care what the court thinks of me? Honestly, you don't know a single thing about me. So what if I left with someone? I have things I have to take care of before I am forced to be your broodmare."

The words Lucifer said echoed in her mind. Her father flinched. Her mother's face remained impassive.

"I don't want to marry Theodus. I don't want to be part of the fae court. I don't want anything to do with you either. If you cared anything about me, you wouldn't force any of that on me."

Her pronouncement hung in the air between the three of them for several long moments. There was a small part of her which regretted saying those things, but she squashed it. They needed to hear the truth.

"What happened to you in Hell? You weren't like this before," her father asked.

"Nothing."

"The man you left with. He has something to do with this, doesn't he?" her mother asked. "Who is he?"

There was no way she was giving up Lucifer's name.

"None of your business."

"Candace, are you in love with someone else?"

She turned away from them, her fists clenched. She wanted to kick them both out. Her heart contracted.

I love Lucifer. He knows and he said nothing.

But he'd made love to her earlier. He'd kissed and touched her with such tender care. If that didn't show he wanted her still, then she wasn't sure what else would. He'd asked her to stay with him more than once. There could be no doubt in her mind.

"So what if I am?" she whispered. "It wouldn't make you change your mind."

Neither of them said anything, but she knew they'd heard her. *Typical.* She turned back to them.

"Are we done? I need to see Theodus if you're going to continue to insist I marry him."

Gwilliana looked as though she would say more, but she turned to Gallian.

"I must return to my court."

She stepped through the portal, but her father didn't follow. He closed the portal.

"Candace, did you meet someone? Is this why you're upset?"

"Who said anything about me being upset?"

Her father sighed, taking a step towards her.

"I can't help you if you won't tell me."

"How can you help? You're the one who bargained with my life in the first place."

"Please, Candace, don't. I know and I'm sorry. All I want is for you to be happy."

"You've got a funny way of showing it."

Fighting with her father was normal, but this felt different.

"Do you really not wish to marry who she picked for you?"

"It's not about that. Theodus is fine, but he's not... he's just not him."

She'd almost said Lucifer's name. Almost. Her father closed the distance between them, tucking a finger under her chin, forcing her face up.

"Are you really in love with this person?"

"Yes, Dad."

What's the use of lying to him?

He frowned, looking her up and down with concern on his face.

"There's something different about you."

"What do you mean?"

Nothing had changed as far as she was aware.

"Why do I sense an otherworldly power on you?"

Now he's just being weird. We're already otherworldly as it is being witches.

"Dad, you're not making any sense."

He put his hands on her biceps, looking her up and down.

"Did someone heal you? What happened? Did you get hurt?"

She stiffened. Her father had always been sensitive to other magic, but this was different.

Can he sense Lucifer's divine power?

How would he know she'd been healed last night? It had been a difficult evening. Being beaten up by two Dukes of Hell was the icing on the cake.

"Dad..."

His eyes roamed down her until he homed in on her leg. There was no time to stop him. He dropped to his knees and tugged up her trouser leg. His eyes grew wide.

"Who gave you this? Who marked you? Who?"

Fuck. I forgot about that.

She hadn't even looked at it herself. She pulled away from him. Walking around him, she moved over to the sofa and sat down. When she pulled up her trouser leg again, her breath caught in her throat.

He's right. It is beautiful.

She traced the line of one of the pairs of wings. Three sixes were wrapped around them in exquisite lettering. It fit Lucifer so well. His dual nature. The angel and the Devil. And now she had a piece of him with her. Even if she could never be with him, this would remind her of their time together. She wanted to cry, but her father's voice brought her back to the present.

"Tell me right now. Who marked you?"

"Who do you think?"

"Is this what happened in Hell? Who did you meet?"

Exhaustion set into her bones. She felt like she'd been fighting for months. Fighting against her attraction to the Devil. Fighting to keep her feelings hidden. Fighting against her duty. All of it had worn her down.

"Lucifer," she whispered.

What's the point in keeping it from him? I'm tired of secrets. I'm tired of everything.

"What? Why on earth would he mark you?"

"Put two and two together, Dad. Who do you think kept me safe when I was there?"

She looked up at her father. His eyes were wide with realisation. She stifled the urge to sigh. All she wanted right then was to run back to Hell and beg him to keep her from this. Even if she still felt awkward after her confession.

He'd protect me. I know he would.

"You... Why... You're in love with him. The Devil."

There we go. Wasn't that hard, was it?

"He's not some evil entity. He's still an angel. I'd appreciate it if you didn't lose your shit with me right now. All of this sucks enough as it is."

He walked over slowly and sat beside her, putting his hand on her shoulder.

"Will you tell me what happened in Hell now?"

"What can I say? I tried not to feel things for him because of my impending wedding. I tried, but he is just everything I never knew I wanted or needed. It hurts so much, Dad. I don't want to marry Theodus. The thought of anyone else but Lucifer being close to me tears me up inside. I don't know how else to explain it. I love him for all that he is."

Two hot, wet tears fell down her cheeks.

"Come here."

He tugged her into his arms, rubbing her back. She sobbed onto his shoulder. It had been a long time since she'd cried in front of her father. Everything caught up with her at once. The pain settled in her chest. The gut wrenching feeling that she'd never be happy without Lucifer.

"It's okay, shh, just let it out."

They stayed like that until her sobbing abated. She pulled away, wringing her hands.

I didn't mean to get so emotional in front of him.

"I hate seeing you in so much pain, knowing I'm partly to blame for your misery. I know you think I'm disappointed in you, but that's simply not the case. I pushed you as a child. I wanted you to reach your full potential. I have never been prouder of you and I'm sorry I ever made you feel otherwise."

He took a clean handkerchief from his pocket. Turning her face towards him, he wiped away her tears. *He's proud of me? What? I don't understand.* Her entire life he'd been cold and aloof. What changed?

"I only want you to be happy. I love you so much. Can you forgive me?"

"Wait, you're not mad?"

"Why would I be? You're free to love who you choose."

"I thought you'd be unhappy since you know, he's an angel and the Devil and all the other crap associated with his name."

He smiled at her, fondness in his expression.

"I promise to be a better father to you. If it means accepting that you want to be with Lucifer, then I can do that."

This was not the sort of conversation she ever expected to have with her father.

"Dad, you know I can't be with him. Not with my marriage to Theodus."

"I need to tell you something."

"What?"

"Your mother is just obsessed with that prophecy. I do not believe she is truly incapable of conceiving with another fae. I think she wants to believe it's fate that I gave her a child of two worlds."

Then I don't need to provide her with an heir if she is capable.

The possibility of her not having to marry Theodus gave her a small sliver of hope.

"What if it's not even related to the fae?"

"I think you are the girl in the prophecy, Candace. I just do not believe it relates to your mother and her need for an heir."

He'd never told her he felt that way. She didn't quite like the idea that she was part of some ridiculous prophecy because she didn't believe in them. Yet, what her father said made sense.

"Then why haven't you stopped her from forcing this on me?"

"I didn't know you had other desires for your life. I want to help you be with the person you choose."

"I don't think I have a choice, Dad. Not now."

He put a hand on her shoulder.

"There is always a choice. You'll see. One way or another, we'll resolve this."

Chapter Twenty One

andace paced the room, clenching and unclenching her fists. The conversation was getting them nowhere.

"Why do you not wish to come live with me?" Theodus asked, pale green eyes fixed on her.

She'd asked her father to bring her here. He was waiting outside the door, in case she needed him. This engagement was a sham and she wanted nothing more to do with it.

"Why? Why? This is merely a marriage of convenience or have you forgotten that already?"

"Is that what it is to you?"

"What else would it be? Do you think I want this? I never wanted to be married off. This is my mother's doing."

"Well, I'm sorry you feel that way, but this is what I want. I want you."

She turned to him, stopping in her tracks.

He what? That's not possible. We barely know anything about each other.

"You can't have me."

The words were out before she could stop them. She was Lucifer's. Putting a hand to her mouth, she looked at Theodus in horror.

"This is about the man from last night, isn't it?"

"No."

"Who is he, Cadmi?"

She flinched at the use of her fae name. *I never want to be called that again.*

"No one."

"Tell me the truth. I am to be your husband. If you wish to be with someone else, then we need to come to an agreement over it."

It took a full minute for her to wrap her head around what he'd just said.

"Are you telling me you would allow me to warm another man's bed whilst married to you?"

She hadn't meant it to come out like that, but it was what he insinuated.

"Do we have to discuss it in such distasteful terms? I am merely telling you I do not expect you to remain faithful to me once we've had a child."

I want a life with Lucifer not Theodus. I would give up everything for him.

The world dropped out from underneath her. It had played on her mind for quite some time. Whether or not she'd have the strength to tell her family no. Whether she'd turn her back on her life on Earth for a life with Lucifer in Hell.

All I want is him. Nothing else matters.

"What if I refuse to give you that?"

"Then I won't allow you to see whoever it is you want rather than me."

Her lip twitched, nails digging into her palms.

"Won't allow me? You don't rule my life. I am not someone you can just dictate terms to."

His pale eyes regarded her with a neutral expression. If he thought she was going to submit to him, he was sorely mistaken. How could her mother think she wished to marry such a man? He was showing his true colours now. Even if she accepted his terms, Lucifer would never allow it. He wouldn't share her.

"I can and I will."

"You know what, fuck you. You can tell my mother I'm done. Done with you, her and her entire court."

Who the hell does he think he is? How can my mother think this man is a suitable match for me?

She was so angry, she could barely contain her fury. It was time to leave. She could see this would never get them anywhere. She didn't get a chance to step towards the door. Theodus descended on her, grabbing her arm and pulling her to him.

"You think we're done? We're not even anywhere close to being done," he said.

His mouth crashed against hers. Bile and revulsion rose in her stomach. His lips weren't soft like Lucifer's. She was too shocked to push him away.

Pain radiated from the mark on her ankle. It tore up her leg. Her skin was burning, on fire. Pink smoke flared out of her hands, slamming into Theodus' chest and pushing him ten feet away from her. She panted, the pain in her leg almost crippling her.

What the fuck? Why does it hurt? What did Lucifer do to me?

"Don't fucking touch me!"

Putting one foot in front of the other, she limped from the room, throwing the door open and slamming it shut behind her. Gallian stood up from the chaise lounge in the hallway, his eyes full of concern. She threw herself down onto his recently vacated seat, pulling up her trouser leg. The mark was no longer black. The lines were bright red and angry. Like he'd burnt her skin with a branding iron.

"What happened?" Gallian asked.

"Theodus is a piece of shit, that's what happened."

He sat down next to her, waving a hand over the mark. White smoke poured from his fingers, soothing away the pain. The mark was still red and raw, but she couldn't feel it any longer.

"Dad, I need you to take me to Hyde Park."

"We need to talk about why that happened."

He pointed at the mark.

"There is only one person I'm going to get answers from about it. Take me to Hyde Park."

Her father sighed before standing and waving his hand again. More smoke poured from his fingertips and the next moment, a purple light shimmered before them. She stood, taking his hand and stepping through the portal. They landed in a secluded area of the park.

"Candace... What did Theodus do?" he asked, putting a hand on her arm to stop her from leaving.

"He suggested after I give him a child, I could go off and be with someone else whilst still remaining married to him. When I told him no, he tried to dictate crap to me, and you know no one tells me what to do. I told him I was done and he kissed me."

159

Except that's not strictly true. Lucifer tells me what to do in the bedroom and I like it. Fuck do I like it when he takes control. When he punishes me for disobedience. I need it. All of it.

"Did the mark start to burn when he kissed you?"

"Yes."

The realisation dawned on her. Lucifer's mark meant more than just him claiming her. He owned her and if anyone else touched her, she'd suffer for it. A part of her was furious, but the other side understood and accepted it. A strange sense of calm descended over her.

"I have to go now, Dad. I'll phone you later. I promise."

He released her arm, letting her walk away. It didn't take her long to find Lucifer's portal to Hell. She'd memorised the location when he brought her home this morning. He'd told her how to activate it. She muttered the words and a purple light shimmered in front of her the next instant. She walked through and out into the corridor. Mall was just coming out of her office.

"Oh, hello again," she said.

"Where is he?" Candace asked.

"In the throne room."

"Is he alone?"

"Yes... What's wrong?"

Candace shook her head, striding towards the throne room. There was no time to explain to Mall nor did she want to. This was between her and Lucifer alone.

"Don't let anyone disturb us."

She didn't wait for Mall to respond. She threw the door open. Lucifer sat on his throne, his chin propped up on his hand whilst he looked down at his tablet. His gaze flicked up to her, eyes widening a little. The door slammed shut behind her. She walked over to him, up the stairs before she knelt at his feet, her head bowed and her hands folded in her lap.

"Candace, what are you doing?"

"I need to be punished."

"What?"

"You need to punish me."

"Get off the floor and look at me. What are you talking about?"

There was no going back from this now. She'd known the minute she realised what Lucifer's mark signified.

"No. I am yours. I was reminded of that very fact today when Theodus kissed me because you claimed me. Marked me. Branded me as yours. I let someone else touch what's yours. I have denied you, made you wait, made you suffer because I kept saying no. I'm asking you to do what you promised me that first night I asked you to stay with me. I want you to hurt me. To punish me because I deserve it."

The silence permeated the air for several moments. He stood, stepping around her. His fingers trailed over her shoulder before he stopped behind her. The atmosphere between them changed in an instant. Lucifer wouldn't hold back. Not when she'd offered herself to him willingly. It was always about consent between them. He needed her to submit to him.

"Get on all fours and place your hands on the throne, after which you will not move until I say so."

She didn't hesitate, crawling towards the throne and placing her hands on the seat, palms flat. She heard the click of his fingers. Her clothes were gone, leaving her bare before him. He trailed something up her back, around her neck until it rested on her cheek. She looked down at the end of the riding crop. *Fuck.* The thought of him using it on her made her blood pound in her ears.

"Did it hurt when he touched you?"

He removed the crop from her face, trailing it back down her spine. She shivered, the anticipation causing heat to pool between her thighs.

"It burnt."

"Good."

She felt the first slap across her behind. It stung, but she didn't flinch away.

I asked him to punish me. I asked for all of this.

He quickly followed it up by several more, each one stinging as much as the last.

"Did you like that prince kissing you?"

Another strike. Her skin felt like it was on fire.

"No. I'll never let him come near me again. Not after what he said."

The crop trailed up her sex before she felt the sharp sting of it against her core. She whimpered, biting down on her lip. Pain radiated from all of the places he'd struck her.

"And what did he say?"

"He hinted if I was to give him a child, he'd turn a blind eye to me seeing other people."

The crop ran down her inner thigh.

"Did you tell him about me?"

"No. He saw us together before we left, so he knows there's someone else in my life."

He nudged her legs further open with his foot. She wanted to look back at him. See his expression. He'd told her not to move and she'd obey.

"Who do you belong to?"

The crop ran along her behind. He struck again. A moan of pain and pleasure escaped her lips. Four more strikes radiated across her behind.

"You."

The sharp intake of his breath echoed through the room. He struck her along her back, making her hiss.

More. I want more.

"Mmm, do you know how sexy you look right now? Perfectly pliant."

The sound of something clattering on the floor followed by his fingers running across her heated skin made her whimper.

"Fuck, Candace. You make me so hard. You haunt my every moment with thoughts of hurting you, marring your perfect skin, fucking you and soothing all the pain away when I'm done."

His dark desires called to her. She'd never known what she really needed. The man behind her was it. He leant down and kissed each mark. Every touch of his lips made her heart pound faster. Her core ached. She wanted him filling her. Fucking her with no mercy.

"Do you want me?" he whispered, his voice soft, seductive.

"Yes," she whimpered.

"How much do you want me?"

His fingers trailed up her inner thighs.

"I can't stand it. Every time you touch me, my skin feels like it's on fire. I ache for you. Please, please, Lucifer, please."

162

He stopped short of brushing against her sex. A whimper of frustration tore out of her mouth.

Holy fuck. I've never been so turned on and desperate for another person in my whole life.

"I want you to promise me something."

Whatever it was, she'd agree. She'd do anything for him. Give up her life if it meant she could be by his side.

"Promise you'll never leave me. I need you."

He needs me? Shit, Lucifer.

His confession sent her over the edge. She'd lay down her life for him. Give him all he desired.

"I promise."

As if I would ever leave now.

"Tell me how you feel. I want the truth."

His hand ran up her back and curled around her throat, fingers tightening on her neck in an almost painful grip. She'd said it once. Could she say it again?

"Lucifer, please."

"Tell me."

His hand tightened, almost cutting off her airway.

"Let me say it to your face," she rasped. "Please."

She needed to see his reaction. It was too impersonal with him behind her. His grip relaxed a little. His other hand cupped her sex.

"Even after everything you went through last night, you still let me hurt you."

She wanted to scream it at him. Tell him it was because he had all of her. Her body. Her mind. Her heart. Even her soul.

"Look at me."

His hand was still around her neck, but she turned her head back. His dark eyes were hazy with lust. Her submission fed him. She could see all his thoughts laid bare to her.

I am everything to him. Everything he needs.

She parted her lips, needing to get the words out before she lost her nerve entirely.

"You are the world to me. You give me everything I have ever needed. You own me. All of me. Even the things I thought I'd never give to another person, I give to you willingly."

His expression darkened. A hot wave of desire drove through her when his fingers sunk into her heated sex. He growled. His fingers weren't enough. She wanted to feel him, pressed deep inside her. Filling her up to the hilt.

"I want the whole truth, my little witch."

She stared into those mesmerising eyes for a full minute. There was nothing holding her back. There was no embarrassment. All she felt was the connection between them she craved with every breath she took.

"I love you."

Chapter Twenty Two

The look in his eyes almost cleaved her in two. His fingers twitched on her throat. Understanding, acceptance and sinful desire radiated off him in waves. He extracted his fingers from her. She felt the loss keenly. He unbuckled his belt, tearing open his fly and sunk into her.

Shit. Fuck. He feels so good.

He grunted, fingers tightening around her airway.

"Say it again. Tell me again."

"I love you."

He pulled back and slammed into her. The force of it sending shockwaves down her back.

"Again."

How many times is he going to make me say it? Is this getting him off?

She wanted to give him what he needed. If that was her admitting her feelings to him over and over again then she would.

"I love you, Lucifer."

He growled, the sound rumbling in his chest. His other hand gripped her hip, keeping her anchored to him.

"Do you want me to fuck you with no mercy, Candace?"

"Yes, I need it."

His fingers dug into her hip. Each thrust was harder than the last. Each grunt from his mouth echoed through the room. The sound of their skin slapping together permeated the air. Her whimpers grew louder.

"I want to hear you scream. Show me how much you like it when I fuck you."

She let it rip, her throat burning from the sound emitting from her lips. He was still half cutting off her airway with his fingers, but she stopped caring. The dark, wild look in his eyes caused her to clench around him, over and over. He was going to send her rocketing over the edge if he wasn't careful.

"You're not allowed to come yet," he told her. "Not until I say so. Not until I've fucked you so hard, you won't be able to walk straight."

She was relatively sure he'd already whipped and fucked her hard enough to achieve that. Only his hands on her kept her from collapsing in a heap on the floor. He let go off her neck, gripping her other hip. The force of his pounding rattled her teeth. She took several gulping breaths, forcing oxygen back into her lungs. She'd never been fucked so brutally in her life. Even when he'd spanked her last night, it didn't compare to this.

"Fuck, you're so hot and tight. You're mine. Mine. Fuck. I need you. I fucking need you and it fucking hurts when you go back to Earth and leave me here alone. I fucking care. Do you understand? I care about you. No one has ever made me want to offer them everything. I want to beg you never to leave me again. Get down on my fucking hands and knees and beg."

Those words caused her heart to constrict painfully in her chest. She knew what it cost him to admit those things to her.

"I love you," she whispered.

"Tell me you'll stay."

I want to. I want to so much, but I have things to take care of. Soon. I promise you soon I'll be able to give you what you want.

If only she could say it, tell him she'd give up everything for him.

"Please believe me when I tell you I love you. I want you. I need you. Only you. Just give me time."

He growled, slamming into her harder.

"Stop saying no to me. I'll hurt you again if you say no. I won't stop punishing you."

"It's not no. I'm not saying no."

How could she make him understand she needed to settle things with her mother and with Theodus before she could be his fully? She couldn't just leave without being able to talk things through with her father. And there was still Jax, she needed to have it out with him. There was so much she had to do.

"I promise I'll be with you. I'm yours. Please, let me deal with my present so you and I can have our future."

He released her hips, grabbing a hold of her shoulders and pulling her up, flush with his chest. His fingers trailed over her stomach, his mouth right next to her ear.

"Do you need me as much as I need you?" His voice was soft, breath fanning across her cheek.

"*Te amo, Lucifer. Anima tua.*" *I love you, Lucifer. My soul is yours.*

She rarely spoke Latin unless it was for spell crafting. If he wasn't going to listen to her in English, then perhaps he would take her seriously now. His fingers trailed lower until they brushed over her core.

"*Vos anima mea,*" he replied. *You are my soul.*

Tears welled in her eyes. He hadn't exactly told her he loved her back, but what he had said meant more to her than those three words.

His soul and mine are entwined.

"I will give you time," he whispered. "Keep your promise to me."

There were no more words. He thrust up into her over and over again, forcing her into accepting all of him as his fingers swept over her core. It sent jolts up her spine, but she held back, keeping a leash on her desperate need to find a release. He hadn't said she could come.

He cupped her chin, forcing her face back and kissing her. It was gentle, his tongue sweeping over hers. His tenderness was unexpected.

"*Come all over me, my little witch. Let me feel you.*"

The sweet release came moments later, tearing through her body, transporting her to somewhere she'd never been before. It was as if her soul had transcended to a higher place. Sparks formed in her vision. She could barely get enough oxygen into her lungs whilst it took hold, washing over every inch of her skin with exquisite bliss.

She cried out his name. The harsh growl in her ear only made her spiral higher. Her hands gripped his arm around her waist, fingers and nails digging into his skin. There was nothing but the two of them. All she could feel was him wrapped around her, keeping her upright.

Her head lolled on her chest when the trembles and aftershocks subsided. She was spent. Her skin stung in the places he'd hit her with the crop, but she couldn't bring herself to give a damn. All she wanted was to curl up against his chest and fall asleep.

My angel. My devil. My Lucifer.

He'd told her she owned his soul. It never occurred to her that he might belong to her as she did to him until now.

"Are you really mine?" she whispered.

He pressed a kiss to her shoulder.

"Yours. Hmm... perhaps, my little witch."

He is mine. I don't need him to tell me if he's not ready to admit it.

"If you let me go, I think I'll collapse."

He chuckled, the sound echoing around her skull. He swept her up into his arms and stood. Her head rested against his chest. She closed her eyes, savouring his warmth on her bare skin. She placed her hand on his chest, feeling his heart thudding erratically. He carried her from the room.

When she opened her eyes again, they were in his bedroom and he'd placed her on his bed. He clicked his fingers, his clothes disappearing in an instant. Her mouth went dry at the sight of him.

Fuck. I will never get over how stunning he is.

"I can feel your desire from here," he said. "Have you not had enough?"

"If you heal me, I can take whatever you have to offer."

His lips curled up at the side, mesmerising dark eyes twinkling with mischief. Kneeling on the bed, his hands ran up her sides. She could feel his power washing over her skin. The sting of his whipping faded.

"You already wear my brand. No need to wear the evidence of my passion for you all over your delicate skin."

She grabbed his hand, pulling him down towards her. Kissing him with tenderness, her fingers curled into his hair.

I want to wear your passion. I want everyone to know I am yours. I don't want secrets anymore. I'm not hiding how I feel about you.

He pulled away only to settle next to her and tug her into his arms.

"Mmm, tell me again what it is you feel."

"How many times do I have to tell you until you believe me?"

"Who said I didn't believe you."

She raised her head from his chest, staring up at him.

"Do you trust me?"

His fingers brushed over her cheek, adoration in his expression.

"With all that I am."

Her heart did several backflips in her chest.

"My heart, my body, my soul is yours. I love you."

"You didn't have to come all this way with me," Candace said.

Lucifer stared down at the woman who utterly enraptured him, took his heart and soul and made it her own. Memories of her on her knees before him, asking him to punish her assaulted his senses. He struggled to maintain a straight face. Her skin had been red, bloody bruises all over her luscious behind from where he'd struck her.

Fuck, all I want is to tear her clothes off again. When will it ever be enough?

"Are you paying attention to what I'm saying?"

Her voice brought him up short.

"Sorry, what did you say?" he replied, running a hand through his hair.

Tamping down on his insatiable need to have her, he reached for her. She let him tug her closer.

"I said don't you have Hell to rule?"

"I already made an example of my subjects. No one will dare step out of line now. You are more important."

Her eyes roamed down the length of him before they stopped short at the unmistakable bulge.

"Are you thinking about what happened yesterday?"

Her tongue ran across her bottom lip.

"How can I not?"

"Well, now isn't the time for sex and punishment. You can have all of that later when I come home."

His heart slammed against his ribcage.

Home. Is my home hers too?

She'd confessed all her feelings to him, but he still wasn't sure she was really prepared to stay with him in Hell.

"I don't always wish to punish you, my little witch. You didn't complain earlier."

Her cheeks stained red.

Mmm, I worshiped every inch of her body with my tongue. I made love to her. Vanilla with her is just as exquisite as whipping her perfect skin and fucking her without restraint.

"Quit it. I can't focus with you saying those things and looking at me like you want to devour every inch of me. I need to decide who I speak to first."

That's why he'd brought her back to Earth. She wanted time to resolve everything. And he didn't want her to have to go through it all alone.

"Perhaps you should start with the easiest conversation."

"That would be Dad. After all, when I talk to my mother, it means cutting all ties with the fae."

He cupped her cheek, noticing the turmoil in her eyes. What he was asking wasn't easy for her. She'd told him everything last night, not leaving out any details. She looked down at their feet.

"And, well, Dad kind of told me he wants to meet you. You don't have to or anything."

He tucked a finger under her chin, forcing her face upwards. Her violet eyes were full of caution.

"Are you afraid to ask me for things?"

"No, I'm not scared of you. It's just well, this isn't exactly the most normal relationship. I mean it's not as if I'm your equal. You're an angel and well, I'm me. And—"

He put a finger over her lips, silencing her.

She doesn't half look young when she's flustered.

For a minute, he wondered if he was really doing the right thing by asking her to stay with him. She might love him now, but would that last? Would she be able to handle a life in the darkness with him?

"Candace, do you need a human term for what this is?"

She nodded against his finger.

"You are my lover. You are etched on my soul, my little witch."

She swallowed, staring up at him with surprise written all over her face. He smiled.

She is beautiful and innocent of so much.

He dropped his hand.

"Oh. Well, I can't tell my father I'm your lover. He said he's on board with this, but that might not fly with him."

A bark of laughter erupted from his mouth. She grinned. He leant down towards her, stealing a kiss from her lips. It sent a wave of longing through him.

Fuck. I need to have her before her father comes here or I won't be able to control myself.

His hands cupped her face and he backed her away to the sofa. She squeaked in surprise when he pressed her down onto it.

"What are you doing?"

"I need to fuck you, now."

"Lucifer!"

"Shh, unless you want me to have a raging hardon for you when your father is here, I suggest you be quiet and let me."

Her eyes went wide, hand curling around his back.

"Does that mean you'll meet him?"

"Yes, did you think I wouldn't agree? I do want to steal his daughter away to Hell."

He leant down, kissing her neck. She arched up into him.

"I'd hardly call it stealing when I agreed to come willingly."

"Mmm, so submissive and pliant. I wonder what else you'll let me do to you without complaint. There is so much you don't know about pleasure and pain."

He bit down, causing her to cry out. Her fingers dug into his back.

"I want your skin blossoming for me. I love your screams, your moans, your whimpers."

"I'll do anything you want. You know that."

Her voice was breathy, her pulse spiking. What he would give for time to stand still so he could fuck her until she bled for him. He tore open her blouse, buttons skating across the floor.

"You have the most perfect skin."

He leant down, freeing her breast from her bra and biting down hard on her nipple. Her fingers threaded in his hair. He loved her touching him. He wanted her hands all over him. Next time, he'd let her have control, but for now, he wanted her submission.

"Please, don't tease. I need you," she moaned. "Fuck me."

Oh, I will, my little witch. I'll fuck you until you can't take it and then I'll fuck you some more. It's time you understand what belonging to me really entails.

Chapter Twenty Three

 *L*ucifer leant against the dining room table, eying Gallian whilst Candace made tea for her father in the kitchen. He could see the faint resemblance between them. She had Gallian's nose and the same sharp intelligence radiated from behind both their eyes.

"So, you're who my daughter cannot stay away from," Gallian said, leaning back on the sofa.

Candace gave both of them a warning look.

She's telling me to play nice. As if I wouldn't.

"All I ask is that you take care of her," her father continued. "Make sure she's happy."

All he wanted was to make his little witch happy. She didn't always know what she needed, but he'd be there to show her. His eyes drifted over the sofa. Only half an hour ago, he had her pinned down, his head between her legs.

Fuck, she tastes incredible. I need to get my mind out of the gutter, but fuck, if she doesn't make me want her all the time.

"I assure you, I care for Candace and will protect her."

Her violet eyes met his. They shone with appreciation and love. He'd never get over how open and willing she was when it came to him. How much she cared. And most of all, that she loved him.

I'm not worthy of her love or affection for me. I'm selfish. Selfishly wanting her with me when her home is on Earth.

"I'm just making sure. It's not every day your daughter tells you she wants to forsake her duty and run off into the sunset with the Devil."

"Dad!"

Lucifer smirked. Her father was merely trying to get a rise out of him. Candace was well aware that a life with him wasn't going to be sunshine, romance and roses. He dealt in sin and punishment.

"She will be safe and cared for."

Candace brought two mugs with her, giving one to her father. She looked between the two men, her expression conflicted. He put a hand out to her. She stepped towards him, holding the mug to her chest. He wrapped an arm around her waist, his hand clinging to her possessively.

That's right, my little witch, you belong by my side. Now and always. Mine. You belong to me.

He'd already spent enough time away from her. His need for her would never be sated.

"Dad, she's going to be pissed when I tell her," she said.

"Do you expect anything less from your mother?" Gallian replied.

"No. I never felt connected to the fae so it doesn't matter. It's just I won't be able to come back until it's blown over."

She looked up at Lucifer, her eyes full of hesitation. This is why he wanted to be by her side. No matter how strong and assured she was, Candace was still fragile inside. She'd been denied her parents' affection and approval for so long.

He'd begun to understand what drove her. The feelings of neglect and hurt which rested deep inside her soul. She'd told him she saw all his damaged parts. He saw hers too. And yet they loved each other all the same. He'd have the courage to tell her soon. When he knew she'd given up the last of her ties to this world for him.

"I won't be able to return to Earth for the foreseeable if I do this," she finished.

"Is this your way of telling me you've agreed to return to Hell?" her father asked.

She turned to him. Lucifer could see her fingers tightening around the mug.

She's preparing herself for his disappointment. Fuck.

He wanted to soothe away her fears. Teach her that she was worthy. That she didn't need her father's approval.

"You know how I feel, Dad. I want... I need..."

His hand tightened around her waist.

You can do this. You can tell him the truth, my little witch.

"I'm choosing this because it's what I want. No one is forcing me. I want my life to be my own for once. Without all the expectations and duties hanging over my head."

She trembled. He could feel her conviction flooding through her veins. He'd asked her to stay, made her promise not to leave him, but it wasn't with force. He needed her willingness and she'd given it to him. Given him everything. And he'd give her all he was in return when she came home free of the shackles keeping her tethered to Earth.

"Candace, I only wish you to have your heart's desire. I told you yesterday, I will do anything in my power to make up for bargaining with your life."

The urge to growl and rip her father a new one drove through him. Only the woman anchored to his side stopped him. Her father had sold his own daughter's life, but he was also the only family Candace would have left who cared for her.

Her eyes snapped to his as if she could feel tension radiating off him. She wanted access into his thoughts. Her expression told him that much. He wasn't about to kiss her in front of her father. He'd break and want to take out his anger on her delicate skin.

Red, hot, painful lust spiked in his blood.

Fuck. She has no fucking clue how much I need to use her, hurt her, ruin her. Fuck, I shouldn't take out my pain on her.

Pain. It lanced through his chest. The pain of never being able to return to Heaven. The pain of being cast out for wanting freedom. The pain of the shackles his father had placed on him when he'd been consigned to rule Hell. All of it sliced through him, threatening to overflow.

What the fuck is this?

It had been a long time since he'd felt anything but rage, hatred and a need for revenge when it came to his father.

Candace's expression softened. She reached up, placing her hand on his heart for a moment. Her eyes said 'I know you're suffering with things I can't change but let me love you and share your burdens'.

175

Fuck if it doesn't make me more aware of how much I don't deserve her and how much I love her all the same.

She knew the pain of parental disappointment. And she'd willingly sacrificed her life to belong to him. He held something so precious, so unbelievably pure of sins.

It was then he knew.

When Candace faded from this world, his father would take her away from him because her soul, which she'd given to Lucifer, belonged in Heaven.

Despite all the pain he felt at the loss of his home and his father's approval, he knew losing her would be the worst fucking pain of all. It almost robbed him of his control and his anger at his father threatened to spill over.

"Lucifer, I'm here, stay with me," she whispered.

Her voice shattered him. She had no clue how dark his thoughts were yet her words were exactly what he needed.

She's here and she's mine.

He shook himself, dispelling the violence locked inside him. The need to destroy his father dulled.

He brushed her hair from her cheek, giving her a haunted smile. Her tentative returning one spoke volumes. She wasn't going to rest until she'd torn his pain to shreds and made him admit to what tormented his very existence.

She is more terrifying than any sort of punishment my Father might exact. She has the power to ruin me if she leaves me. She'll break my heart.

No one had ever had such power over him before. He could only hope her love for him was enough to keep her by his side.

He turned back to her father. Gallian's expression held curiosity and understanding. As if he realised what tethered Lucifer to his daughter.

Love.

Would it keep her father happy, knowing Candace was everything to him?

Gallian stood, walking over and placing his mug on the dining room table. He took the mug from Candace and placed it next to his. Taking her shoulders in his hands, he smiled at her.

"You'll have some way of staying in contact with me."

He looked over at Lucifer who nodded his assent. Now the portals had reopened, there was nothing standing in the way of her talking to her father.

"Then I'll be content in the knowledge that you're safe with him."

He leant down, placing a light kiss to his daughter's forehead.

"I love you, my child. I will always be proud of you. Remember what I said about everything yesterday. You'll work out what it means for you."

Lucifer frowned, unsure of what Gallian was referring to, but Candace seemed to know.

"Thank you, Dad. I love you too."

Candace sat in the corner of Fright Night with Jax. Both of them were silent. He eyed the vampires in the bar with irritation.

"Say something, Jax."

"What do you want me to say? First, you tell me you're going to marry some fae prince and we won't be able to see each other often and now, you're telling me you've fallen in love with the Devil and you're going to return to Hell, permanently. What the fuck do I say to that?"

She flinched, wishing she hadn't told Lucifer she'd be okay seeing Jax alone.

I knew he'd be pissed, but now I just feel like the world's worst friend.

She'd tried her best to explain everything to him in a way he might understand.

"I thought you'd be happy I was finally honest with you."

"Happy? I'm not fucking happy. You've avoided me since we returned to Earth and now you drop that bombshell on me like it's no big deal."

"I never said it wasn't a big deal," she muttered.

She knew telling Jax wasn't going to be easy, but the way he looked at her as if she'd completely torn him to shreds made her heart ache. There was nothing more she wanted than for all of this to go away and for them to go back to the way they'd always been. She knew that would never happen, not after he'd sent her to Hell. The vast chasm between them widened significantly.

"I don't understand how you can give up your entire life, everything you've ever known for... him."

Is that how he saw it? Her giving up everything? That was ridiculous. She'd made this choice by herself. Even if Lucifer had asked her to stay with him in Hell a thousand times over, it wouldn't have mattered if she hadn't wanted to. She wasn't giving up anything. She was gaining everything she never knew she needed. A man who was so complex it gave her whiplash with his ever changing moods. She accepted Lucifer for all he was regardless. Loved him for it. She still had so much to learn about what made him tick, but none of that mattered.

"Can you not see this is the one choice I've been able to make without someone forcing it on me? Finally taking back control of my life from my parents. Besides, Theodus is a prick and I deserve more than that."

"And you think he's any better?"

"What did you just say?"

"Come on, Candace, you're talking about someone whose job it is to punish souls who have sinned. I wouldn't even like to count the number of shitty things he's done in his existence."

She clenched her fists under the table.

Where does he get off saying shit like that? Does he think I'm unaware of what type of man Lucifer is? Does he even know me at all?

"So what, Jax? So fucking what. Do you think that means he doesn't deserve me?"

"No one will ever deserve you."

She almost reeled back. She hadn't listened to Lucifer or her father about Jax having feelings for her, but she saw them clear as day in his expression now. How had she not realised this before?

"And you think you do?" she whispered.

He had the decency to look away, eyes full of regret. Her chest constricted painfully.

All this time. All this fucking time. Why? Why, Jax? This isn't fair.

She'd never once looked at him as anything other than a brother figure. They'd grown up together. The thought of Jax seeing her as more made her stomach turn.

"What about Sam? Are you just stringing her along?"

"No. I love Sam."

"Then what the fuck? How long have you felt this way about me?"

He let out a long, heart breaking sigh.

"Since we were kids."

She didn't even want to scream and rage at him. She wanted to cry. Betrayal crept into her heart. Her best friend had lied to her face for years. Their entire friendship felt tainted. A wave of nausea rushed through her. She put a hand to her mouth, standing up abruptly.

"Candace?"

She shook her head, backing away and running towards the toilets. The minute she slammed into a cubicle, the tide erupted. She could only be glad she'd braided her hair earlier so it wasn't hanging in her face.

She sat back against the wall when she'd emptied her stomach, feeling completely drained.

There was nothing she could say to her best friend that would make anything better. How could she even face him again? Knowing he was in love with her. Knowing that he'd spent their lives hoping she'd see him as something other than her best friend.

What did he think would happen if I married Theodus? Is that why he tried to save me?

Everything he'd done for her was suddenly unpalatable. He could've had an ulterior motive. Her head started to hurt as all the possibilities ran through it.

I don't want to think about this anymore.

She tugged her phone out of her pocket and sent a text.

Please come get me.

She didn't care if he said I told you so, all she wanted was to curl up in his arms and forget this ever happened. She promptly burst into tears, putting her head in her hands.

How could things between her and Jax ever be the same again?

Chapter Twenty Four

The wind ruffled his hair. Sitting up on the roof of Azrael's building, Lucifer surveyed London with narrowed eyes. He hadn't wanted to leave Candace alone, but she'd insisted.

That boy better not decide it's mutual confession time.

Mall would inform him if anything was amiss in Hell, but things had been quiet. Who knew what kind of plotting was going on between his demons. At that moment, it didn't matter. Provided they didn't do anything too disruptive or involve him, he was content to let them roam as they pleased.

"Are you here because you wish to speak to me?" said a voice from behind him.

"What makes you think this is about you?"

Azrael sat down next to him, his legs dangling off the side. Lucifer wasn't in the mood for talking, but he also didn't want to fight with his brother.

"This is still where I stay when I visit Earth. I've been watching you."

"Then you know what I'm doing here."

The other angel put his hand out.

"Surveying the world now you're free?"

"Freedom came at a cost." *My heart. My heart was the biggest cost of them all.*

"Doesn't it always when it comes to our Father?"

Lucifer bit his lip on a retort. *Our damn Father.* The crux of everything. He looked away, his eyes falling on the buildings in the distance.

"What do you want, Azrael? Shouldn't you be off telling a bunch of humans their time is up? Or have you come here to gloat?"

He didn't much care what his brother wanted. He'd prefer it if Heaven's minions left him in peace.

"Something strange is going on with Father."

He turned his head towards Azrael sharply.

"What do you mean?"

"He is... restless. I've heard Him mutter your name on several occasions. I fear something is amiss."

"Why are you telling me this?"

It didn't make any sense. Why would his brother come to him when their father was up to something?

"Contrary to what you might believe, I hold no animosity toward you. Besides, I thought you might want to know so you could keep... her safe."

So he does know about Candace. I wasn't sure if he'd admit to it or not after he told me he's been watching me.

If Azrael really had no ulterior motives, then he should take the warning seriously. What could his father possibly be restless about?

"Since when did you care about my personal life?"

"You have my wife to thank for that."

"Is that what you're calling her now?"

A stupid human tradition.

He sincerely hoped Candace wouldn't force him into engaging in such an idiotic practice. It wasn't something they'd ever discussed.

Azrael grinned at him.

"No, but I didn't want you jumping down my throat over my 'obsession' with a human."

"The only immortal human in existence you mean."

Lucifer didn't like it. It was all very well having creatures such as vampires technically being immortal unless you staked them, but humans? He'd never done that for anyone before. It wasn't jealousy he felt, surely?

Fuck, I'm not jealous. That's ridiculous. She'll live hundreds of years so I don't have to worry about that now.

But he did. The thought of not having her was like a knife to his heart. Lifetimes passed in his world within a blink of an eye. Why did he have to feel this way about her? Feelings never sat well with him.

I miss her and she's only been away from me a couple of hours. I've fallen foul of emotions.

Emotions.

Feelings.

Those were human things.

He didn't like feeling human. He was an angel. And yet, it was Candace. How could he regret falling in love with the girl who soothed away his pain with a simple look?

"Well, it wasn't as if I asked Him to grant me that. Besides, she's given up most of her life to live amongst angels."

And I'm asking Candace to give up hers to live with demons. How fucking ironic that both of us should find ourselves in a similar situation.

This couldn't be his plan. Did he think his sons needed to be taught how to love? How to care for someone other than themselves? Did it even matter? He was done with God and his plans.

Before he had a chance to answer Azrael, something buzzed in his pocket. He pulled it out.

"Another human contraption," Azrael muttered under his breath.

Candace had given him the phone so she could get in touch with him when she was finished with her friend. There was a single text from her.

Please come get me.

He frowned. Something about it bothered him. She hadn't asked him to go back to her flat. Get her from where? He typed out a response.

Where are you?

A minute ticked by and there was no reply. He looked back up at his brother.

"Where is she, Azrael?"

"Where's who?"

"Candace. I know you can track her down."

Azrael rolled his eyes.

"Still can't hear their thoughts then?"

"No."

Except he could hear hers when they kissed each other. He'd never stopped to wonder why that was, only that it worked in his favour. It was how he discovered her true feelings towards him.

"Fine. Don't know why it's so important you find her now. She's not in danger."

No, but something is wrong.

Azrael went silent for a long moment, his eyes glazing over slightly. It wasn't the first time Lucifer wished their father hadn't taken away his ability to hear human's thoughts. He didn't have time to track her down via her brand nor did he want to hurt her by doing so. It would burn her again, just as it did when that idiotic prince kissed her.

"She's in that vampire owned bar," Azrael said. "The one in Soho."

Lucifer stood, his wings flaring out.

"Before you disappear off. Just be wary of whatever it is Father is planning."

"I'm always wary of our Father and His games. You can never let your guard down when it comes to God."

He didn't wait for a reply, taking to the skies and flying straight towards Soho. He landed outside the steps of the bar, not bothering to hide his actions nor himself from prying eyes.

Let them see the Devil is in their midst for all I care.

He felt her now. She was close. Taking the steps two by two, he shoved the door open and strode past the coat check. The bar wasn't busy. He surveyed it for a moment. The bartender looked up, her eyes going wide the next moment.

"Is that...?" the dark haired vampire whispered.

Ignoring her, he spied Jaxon in the corner, looking sorry for himself.

Where is she?

He strode over, stopping next to the table with Candace's friend. Jaxon almost jumped out of his chair.

"Tell me where she is, now," Lucifer said.

"She ran in the loos," Jaxon said, pointing towards the door. "What are you doing here?"

He didn't bother answering the boy's question, walking away and shoving open the door to the ladies toilets. In one of the cubicles, huddled by the wall was Candace, her head in her hands, sobbing quietly. The sight of it broke him.

What the fuck did that boy say to her?

He knelt down at her feet, putting a hand on her leg. He didn't want to startle her.

"Candace?"

She raised her head slowly. Her eyes were watery and bloodshot.

"You came," she whispered.

"I would've been here sooner if you'd told me where you were."

"I... sorry, I didn't think. Shit."

More tears fell down her cheeks as she hiccupped on a sob. The smell of sick assaulted his nose. He stood, flushing the toilet and grabbing some paper from the holder. He leant down, dabbing her mouth and cheeks. He chucked it away before putting his arms out to her.

"Come here."

He helped her to her feet and bundled her up in his arms, kissing the top of her head. For once, he really did want to be gentle with her. Seeing her so upset made his heart ache.

"Do you want to talk about it?" he asked.

"No," she sobbed. "I just want to leave. Take me back to the flat, please."

He hooked his arm under her legs and picked her up. She wrapped her arms around his neck and buried her face in his chest.

I'll take you wherever you want, my little witch, as long as it makes you happy again. That boy's days are numbered.

All eyes fell on the two of them when he carried her out of the toilets. Jaxon stood up.

"Candace," he said.

Lucifer glared at the boy, striding away. Candace didn't even look up, she just clutched him tighter.

"Well I never," the bartender said quietly. "She was serious about getting with the Devil. Go Candace."

What? Does Candace know this vampire? Did she mention their involvement with each other?

He could ask her about it later. They were out the door the next moment and up on the street. He took to the skies and it wasn't long before they landed outside her flat.

She gave him her keys from her bag, which was slung across her chest. He set her down on her bed when he'd let them both in. She put a hand over her mouth and dashed into the bathroom. The sounds of her hurling her guts up made him follow her.

She looked pale as she sat back after flushing, breathing heavily. He picked up a face cloth from her bathroom sink and wet it. He rang it out before kneeling beside her and wiping her brow.

"Thank you," she whispered. "You shouldn't have to take care of me."

"Why not?"

"I feel like you're always rescuing me."

"You told me I wasn't a knight in shining armour."

"Perhaps I spoke too soon."

He smiled, stroking her hair. She reached up, cupping his face.

"*Te amo.*"

He never wanted her to stop saying 'I love you' for as long as they were together. He couldn't imagine her not looking at him as if he was her everything.

"Let me brush my teeth," she said, dropping her hand from his face.

He helped her to her feet and went into her kitchen, pouring her a glass of water. There was a strange envelope on her counter. He stared down at it. It gave him an ill sense of foreboding.

A moment later, he felt two arms band around his waist and a forehead pressed into his back. He closed his eyes, running his fingers over the backs of her hands.

"I don't care if you don't agree with me," she murmured. "You're mine."

Her possessive tone made him smile.

I'll always be yours, little witch. You stole my heart and you own my soul.

"Are you sure about that?"

"Yes." One of her hands ran down his stomach, coming to rest just above his belt. "If no one else can touch me, those same rules apply to you."

He felt the tingling sensation of her magic. Looking down, he spied pink smoke curling around his belt buckle and tugging it open. There was no doubt in his mind what she was after now.

"I'll hurt anyone who tries," she continued. "They'll wish they never laid eyes on the Devil when I'm done."

"Is that so? A rather bold claim."

She tugged his shirt out of his trousers, tucking her hands underneath and trailing them along the bare skin of his stomach. His muscles tensed.

"You might be able to stop me using magic, but that doesn't apply to others."

Her assertiveness was too much of a turn on. He was rock hard and wanted to fuck her against the counter.

As much as I adore her hands on me, I should make her talk about what that boy said.

"Mmm, you're welcome to use it on me for pleasure, little witch."

Those were not the words he meant to say. Pink smoke trailed up his torso before his shirt was ripped open. Her magic against his skin tingled, brushing over his chest with the gentlest of touches. She ran her fingers up his arms, tugging off both his jacket and shirt. Her breath against his back was quickly replaced by her mouth.

"Candace," he hissed.

"Not going to tell me I have to do as you say?"

He shuddered involuntarily when she ran a hand over him. Her fingers curled around his cock.

"No," he replied, almost breathlessly. "You said I'm yours, so perhaps you should use me as you please."

She'd started this game and now, he never wanted her to stop.

Fuck, I want her on her knees, staring into my eyes with her mouth wrapped around me, taking it all.

Memories of when he'd forced her to that first time almost made him groan.

"Turn around."

He stilled, staring down at that envelope again. It bothered him. He needed to stop this and get her to read whatever was inside it.

"There's something for you here."

She let him go.

"Don't care. Turn around."

"You can do with me what you wish after you've looked at this."

She let out a long frustrated sigh.

"Lucifer, I want to wrap my lips around your cock before I push you down on my bed and ride you. Is it really more important than either of those things?"

Fuck. No. It's most definitely not.

Hearing her tell him she wanted to suck him off made his blood pound in his ears. He picked up the envelope anyway, turning around and holding it out to her. Her cheeks were flushed, her violet eyes dark with unconcealed desire, lust, love.

She looked down at what was in his hands. The blood drained from her face. She snatched it from him, ripping open the envelope and looking down at the embossed card. Her eyes scanned over it. She said nothing, reaching around him and slamming it back down on the counter.

"What is it?" he asked.

She didn't answer. Her hands shot out pressing him back against the counter before she tugged at the zip of his trousers. She had him freed the next moment, dropping to her knees, she did exactly what she told him she wanted to do. Wrapped her lips over him, her small hand curling around the base. And she sucked hard, making him groan.

Fuck. Little witch. I can't fucking think straight.

Chapter Twenty Five

*L*ucifer's hands curled into her hair, encouraging her to slide her lips over him and take more.

"Fuck," he grunted.

She looked up at him.

Shit, she is sexy as fuck on her knees, worshipping me.

Her violet eyes flickered with anger, but he imagined it wasn't directed at him. She took him in long, drawn out strokes of her mouth. All he wanted was to bury himself down her throat.

"Little witch, you're going to make me come quickly if you keep that up."

She smiled, her lips wrapped around him, increasing her pace.

Fuck, that's exactly what she wants.

Her teeth grazed over him. He shuddered, fingers digging into her scalp.

"More, fuck, Candace, take it all."

He gripped the back of her head. Her pretty lips were already halfway down his length, but it wasn't enough. She tilted her head up slightly and he hit the back of her mouth. Slowly, he inched down her throat until she almost choked.

Her eyes weren't panicked. She stroked his thigh, encouraging him to fuck her in the way he clearly wanted to. He groaned, thrusting in and out her throat until the intensity had him pulling back. She released him entirely, taking several deep gulps of air.

"Shit," she muttered.

Sarah Bailey

Before he had a chance to ask her what was wrong, she took him again. Gone was any need to tease. Within minutes, he gripped the counter and cursed several times.

"Little witch," he grunted.

His body tensed, the pleasure riding over him in waves.

Fuck, she knows how to drive me fucking crazy.

When the last pulses faded, she pulled away, standing up.

"You have no idea how much it turns me on having your cock in my mouth. I need to fuck you. Now."

Barely giving him time to register what she'd said, she launched herself at him. Her mouth met his, her kiss electrifying. Her fingers tangled in his hair.

"I'm so fucking angry. How dare she invite me to a fucking dinner in honour of my fake engagement. Fuck her. I'm not marrying that piece of shit. After all that crap with Jax, this is the last thing I need. Fuck. My heart fucking hurts. How could he lie to me about his feelings? All this fucking time. Fuck you, Jax. Damn it. I'm fucking angry and yet I'm so fucking turned on I can barely think straight. I'm so fucked up. I need him in me, like right fucking now so I can lose myself for one minute."

The onslaught of her thoughts made him freeze. He pulled away, holding her shoulders so she couldn't capture his mouth again. She panted, staring up at him with confusion.

"Your mother invited you to a dinner?"

"Yes, fuck, you heard me. I forgot about that."

She ran a hand through her hair.

"Can't you see I need you? If only you could feel how wet I am. Fuck, seriously, Lucifer, I fucking ache right now. Please, let me fuck you and then I'll talk."

The pleading notes in her voice broke through all his concerns.

Just how wet is she? I need to know.

He took her hand, tugging her into the bedroom with him.

"Where do you want me?" he asked.

"Bed and no clothes."

He grinned, obliging with a click of his fingers as he lay down. Her eyes roamed over him with unconcealed desire.

"Fuck, every time I look at you, I get so wet, so fucking turned on," she whispered.

"Do you want to show me how turned on you are?"

Her eyes snapped to his.

"Oh, you'll see soon enough."

She crawled over him, taking one of his hands and shoving it above his head.

"I know you'll be able to get out of this, but let me do this my way. Just this once."

"I'll let you have your way many times over if it means you'll suck my cock like that again, little witch. Just say the word."

Pink smoke curled out of her fingers. When it dissipated, two lengths of rope lay in her free hand. She placed one of them down on the bed beside them before she laced the rope around his wrist and tied him to one of the metal poles on her headboard. She took his other hand, doing the same with that one. He stared up at her with a grin.

"Tying me up? That's a little kinky."

She leant down, her breath tickling his ear.

"I think you're the king of kink with your desire to restrain and whip me until I'm panting and writhing beneath you, begging you to fuck me."

He tested the restraints. She certainly knew how to tie a knot, but he wouldn't try and escape regardless. Tonight was about giving her what she needed and if that was him at her mercy, then he'd oblige until she was ready to talk.

"You won't like not being able to touch me, Lucifer. I'm going to make you beg. Maybe I'll say yes if you please me."

She pulled away, winking at him before jumping off the bed. He bit his lip. Candace wasn't holding back. He'd opened her eyes to a new world of sexual pleasure. He knew she'd never let anyone hurt her before. Now, she wanted his pain because it got her off.

Their dark desires called to each other. The whirlwind of lust caught them up in its storm, rendering it impossible to escape. They'd never be free of each other. He didn't want to be. He wanted to be trapped in her gilded cage forever just as she was in his.

"Tell me, little witch, how long have you fantasised about restraining me?"

"I've fantasised about a lot of things involving you. I intend to make them all a reality."

I bet she has. That mind of hers is always churning away.

Her fingers went to her shirt buttons. She undid them one by one, watching him carefully. Seeing her undress slowly made him ache. He already wanted to beg her to impale herself on his cock so he could feel her heat. Her boots came next, sliding down her shapely legs. Her jeans followed soon after. She stood in lacy pink underwear which did little to conceal her assets from him. Not that he was complaining.

Shit, she has no idea how sexy she is. How her confidence in her own skin makes me want to fuck her so hard. Damn, why did I just agree to allow her to tie me up?

"I don't have to ask if you like what you see, I can tell."

"Are you going to stand there and let me look at you in that all night? Because that'd be just plain cruel."

She laughed, kneeling on the bed and running her hand up his calf. Her touch sent tingles up his spine.

"No, that would be cruel for both of us. I'm going to ride your cock, that's a guarantee, but whether I let you touch me is still up for debate."

"Tell me, what else have you fantasised about?"

She crawled over him, her fingers trailing up his stomach and chest.

"Mmm, would it be terribly naughty of me to want you to fuck me when you're all angelic, wings, halo, everything?"

His lips curved up into a smile.

"I think I'll crown you the queen of kink before the night is over."

"Am I your queen?"

She ran her nails down his chest, the sharp tug of pain made him harder.

She's right. I will be begging her to let me touch her. Fuck.

"You've been my queen since the day we met. The Queen of Hell. Do you want that? Do you want me to make you my equal?"

Her expression changed from lust-filled to shock and confusion. She'd told him they weren't equals, but he didn't see it that way. She was his equal in every sense. Her passion, her fire, her vulnerability, the way she cared.

Everything about her was perfect. Even when she was sometimes cruel and scathing.

Fuck do I love this woman. I would defy my own Father for her if she asked it of me.

"Wh...what?"

"Did I not make the question clear?"

"I... that's... Lucifer, you can't just spring that on me when we're about to fuck. How is that fair?"

He grinned at her.

"All's fair in love and war, did no one tell you that?"

Her nails dug into his chest harder. She leant down, her mouth brushing over his, her violet eyes narrowed. He tried to kiss her, but she kept just out of reach.

"War... I'll draw the battle lines right here," she whispered, capturing his face in her hand, her finger dragging over his bottom lip. "If you want me to kiss you, then you have to ask nicely. Perhaps I'll give you my answer."

The way she'd gone from confused to back in control made his blood pound harder. He imagined her inner monologue wasn't calm and collected.

Quite possibly why she won't kiss me. She can't prevent me hearing what's on her mind.

"You've grown bold, my little witch. It's incredibly sexy. Are you sure you want to continue teasing me? When I break free of these restraints, I won't hold back, unless you like it when I'm rough with you."

"You know the answer to that already."

Her nails ran down his chest, hard enough to almost draw blood. He growled, the sound echoing through the room.

"Tell me where you went when my dad was here. Why did you look so angry and haunted?"

He stiffened under her touch. This was not a subject he wished to discuss with her, especially not when they were playing this game with each other.

"Don't."

"You see, I think you need to talk about what hurts you." Her nails dug harder into his chest. "You told me I'm your everything, that I have your soul, but I don't think you'll ever be free to give me this." She placed her other hand over his heart. "Until you let me in."

That's what she wants? Fuck, Candace, you have that already. I fucking love you so much it physically hurts to be away from you.

"Kiss me, little witch."

"Mmm, you didn't ask nicely."

Her violet eyes caught his, her gaze intense. She wasn't going to take no for an answer nor was she going to give in.

"Please."

Her expression softened. Her mouth hovered over his for a long moment. Her lips brushed against his, gentle and unhurried.

"I want to be your queen, Lucifer. I've laid bare my soul to you. Isn't that enough? Will I ever be enough for you to let me in?"

Her thoughts tore at everything inside him. She was enough. She'd always been enough.

Why would you ever think you weren't? You are my queen.

"Because you won't tell me anything. I live in fear you'll get bored of me and make me leave Hell."

He wanted to curse. How could he make her see sense? He broke off from their kiss.

"Candace, I am yours. Yours. Do you understand? If I could, I'd kneel at your feet and offer myself to you for eternity. I can't fucking live another day without you by my side. I'm deadly serious about making you my Queen of Hell."

He was going to tear out of these bonds if she didn't take him seriously. He looked at her face. Tears pricked at her eyes.

"You just admitted you're mine," she whispered.

"That's because I am. I have been since you landed in my bed and made me fall under your spell. You are my everything. What else do I have to do to prove that to you?"

She sat up, staring down at the deep red marks on his chest she'd made with her nails.

"Just tell me one thing."

"Name it."

"What happened the day He cast you from Heaven?"

He sighed. She just had to push. He had to give her something, if only to prove he trusted her and wanted her in his life.

"If I promise to show you, will you stop this line of conversation and ride my cock? You've made me so fucking hard and I need to be in you."

She was silent for a long moment. She put her hands behind her back, unhooking her bra and tossing it aside. Her underwear followed next. His mouth watered at the sight of her naked above him.

"You want me to fuck you?" she asked.

"I want you so much my cock fucking hurts."

She ground against him, her wetness coating him. He grunted.

Fuck, she wasn't lying. She's soaking.

"Like this, you want me to ride you? Make you come?"

"Fuck, yes," he growled. "Ride my cock, little witch."

She bit her lip, grinding harder. He'd promised he wouldn't try to get free, but he wanted to run his hands over her skin. He wanted to push her down on the bed and fuck her with abandon. Knowing she'd get off on being in control stopped him. She needed to let go. She needed his submission for once.

"I'm going to fuck you, Lucifer, but you don't deserve to touch me. I'm going to make you watch me pleasure myself."

And with that, she shifted and sunk down on him. He groaned.

She's so hot and tight. Fuck, no one compares to her.

She rose and fell slowly, watching him with hooded eyes. She twisted her nipple with her fingers. He watched her, mesmerised by her movements. Not being able to touch her was torture.

She braced one hand behind her as she rode him, her legs open for him to see where they were joined. His heart hammered erratically in his chest. Her fingers trailed down her stomach, brushing against her soft curls before her hand slipped between her legs. She moaned, stroking herself.

"I know you want to touch me here," she said. "Can you feel how wet I am for you? Do you know how much I want to come all over your cock?"

"Little witch," he groaned.

There was nothing he could do but watch her ride him and pleasure herself. Her pace increased, her moaning becoming louder.

Fuck, I'm going to explode in a minute, but I can't come yet, not until I've felt her. I want her clenching around me.

"Tell me, does it make you harder seeing me like this?" she asked.

"Yes, fuck, Candace, please. I want you so fucking much and it kills me that I can't touch you."

"Too bad."

She smiled at him, her fingers moving faster, her hips grinding against him. He growled, thrusting his own into hers. He couldn't help it, he needed to fill her, deeper, harder. Biting her lip, she groaned. He did it again, finding a rhythm to match hers.

"Fuck, Lucifer, I'm going to come all over you, don't fucking stop."

She cried out, shaking and trembling over him as her sex clenched.

Shit, seeing her come apart is so hot.

He tried desperately to hold on, grinding into her. It was too much, he felt the stirring before it ripped through his body.

He cried out her name, falling into oblivion along with her.

Chapter Twenty Six

andace pitched forward onto his chest, panting. He wanted to hold her, run his fingers through her hair, but his wrists were still bound.

"Fuck," she whispered.

"Can I touch you now?" he asked.

She nodded against his chest. The ropes dropped the next instant and he wrapped his arms around her, kissing the top of her head. The battle between them wasn't about winners or losers, it was about love and the need to consume each other.

"Are you really afraid I'll stop wanting you?"

"Only because it scares me how much I love you," she murmured.

His arms tightened around her. Nothing could induce him to let this girl go.

Not now.

Not ever.

"You're the only woman I've given my brand to. Others have worn the sixes, but you wear my wings, little witch. No one else."

She looked up at him.

"I never got a chance to tell you how beautiful it is."

"Just like you, beautiful, strong, so self-assured yet fragile. A bird with clipped wings."

Her eyebrow raised in question.

"Is that supposed to be a metaphor for how I crave my dad's approval and affection?"

"No. They clipped your wings, but I'm showing you how to be free even when you're broken."

She shifted, raising her arms and holding his face in her hands.

"You have shown me more than just freedom. In some crazy, fucked up way, I finally understand myself. I see a girl who thought she wasn't worthy of anything until she met an angel who gave her the one thing she was missing in her life. It was simple. He showed her she always had a choice. That's why that girl now loves without conditions and without restraint. And that's why this angel, right here, will always have her heart."

His heart thumped wildly. The words were on the tip of his tongue. She kissed him before he could say anything.

"I don't need you to love me back. I'm sorry if I pushed you. You don't have to show me anything."

She pulled away, sitting up and staring down at him with those incredible violet eyes of hers.

"I made a promise, little witch. I keep my promises," he said. "But first, you're going to tell me what happened this evening."

Shifting off him, she sat down with her legs crossed. Her fingers traced the outline of his brand.

"My best friend, who I've looked up to as my brother my whole life, told me no one deserves me, especially not someone who punishes people for their sins. He acted like I had no idea of what I was truly getting into by following you home to Hell. That's when I saw the truth. No one will ever deserve me in his eyes, only him. And I swear my heart felt like it'd been tossed in a meat grinder."

She didn't look at him as she spoke. Her eyes filled with tears and her fists clenched in her lap.

"He's lied to my face since we were kids. Everything he's done is tainted by that simple fact. The feeling of betrayal made me sick. It's not as if I've never kept secrets from Jax, but he's kept the biggest one of all from me. It's fucked up that even though he has Sam, he still loves me. I don't see a way through this mess. I suppose that's what hurts the most."

The problem with secrets is someone always got hurt when they all came out. He put a hand on her fist. She looked so lost and scared.

"You're terrified of losing everyone you care for because of your love for me," he whispered.

Her eyes snapped to his. A single tear fell down her cheek.

"Am I really that transparent?"

He shifted turning on his side and propping himself up by his elbow. She opened her fist and he entwined his fingers in hers.

"Not to others, but I've been inside your head, little witch. I know you in ways no one else can. Do you think you're not free to return to Earth as you please? Do you think I'll place restrictions on you?"

"No. I know you won't. I've never had any love for the fae but going against my mother isn't a prospect I relish. And feeling as though I've lost my best friend in the midst of all this when I actually need him on my side. That just plain sucks."

He brushed her hair from her face, wiping away the stray tear. His little witch hurt.

What can I do to make her feel better? Clearly, sex hasn't worked completely.

"What do you need, *animus meus*?" *My soul.*

Her fingers tightened in his for a moment.

"I don't need anything but time, which I'm running out of. My engagement party is next week. I have to face her then."

He let go of her hand, pulling her towards him. She went willingly, curling up against his chest with her hand on his heart.

There was nothing left to say about her problems. It was time he allowed her a little insight into his life.

"I've never spoken of what happened that day except with Azrael, but he was there so that's different."

"You said you were going to show me what happened. How?"

"Close your eyes."

She did as he asked. He placed a hand over them, a soft glow of yellow erupting from his fingertips. Reliving this was never easy, but Candace was right. He had to let her in some day.

She let out a soft gasp, her fingertips pressing into his chest.

He closed his eyes, sucked backwards into a memory he wished he could forget.

The shouting match between Azrael and my father made my head hurt. I couldn't do anything but watch silently. What could I even say? He would never allow us the freedom we desire and now we've angered him.

"You cannot possibly comprehend what servitude means, Father," Azrael said. "You may have created all of this, but you don't understand what you ask of us."

"You are an angel. Your role is to serve."

God. The man who gave us life but put us in chains for eternity. I stepped forward, unable to take the tension between them any longer.

"Stop. Just stop. Do you hear yourself? All of them serve you out of blind allegiance. None of them understand freedom. Azrael and I deserve more. We all do."

My father stared at me with unnerving intensity, but I refused to look away. Azrael walked over, coming to a standstill beside me, his expression hard.

"Is this what we've come to? My sons hating me for their servitude? Or is it because I've put mortals above you?"

I closed my eyes, trying to hold back the tide of curses I wanted to throw at him. He made me so angry, but I needed to remain calm. Unclenching my fists, I opened my eyes and looked at him.

"Neither of us have any love for humans, but that is not why we wish to be free. Choice, Father, that's all we ask. We want a choice to serve, not an edict."

He turned away, pacing the marble floor in front of his chair. It's not quite a throne, carved of white marble, glistening in the light. The other angels who followed us have been punished. Stripped of their current roles and made to serve under those they once presided over. I have no regrets. They wanted freedom as much as Azrael and me.

"You test my patience with every word, Lucifer. Both of you have disappointed me greatly, but you, my brightest son, have hurt me the most. You live in Heaven where you are afforded every privilege imaginable. Why have you defied me at every turn? Do I not do enough for you?"

The words cut me like a knife. He doesn't understand what we are asking of him. Why is choice so difficult for him to wrap his head around? He gave free will to humans, why not to angels? Why are we any different? Just because we are immortal. He says he created us to serve, but I don't believe that for one moment. If we were only meant to serve, he would not have granted us minds of our own.

"Because you put us in chains, Father. They might not be visible, but we are chained nevertheless."

Silence. What else could I ever have expected from him? I looked over at my brother, but his gaze was on our father, undisguised disgust written all over his face.

"Leave us, Lucifer. I will deal with you separately."

I looked at my father one last time before walking out. There is no point arguing. He's made up his mind about what he's going to do with us.

I felt a sense of foreboding. Nothing was right any longer. My life as I know it will change. This was the day everything fell apart.

I paced outside the room for what seemed like eternity, wondering how he'll punish both of us.

Azrael walked out, his head bowed. He didn't look my way as he sat on one of the long benches which looked out over a garden with a fountain in the middle. The water trickled down silently.

"Father says you are to go in now."

"What did he tell you?" *I asked.*

"You know I cannot repeat his words, Lucifer."

I took a breath and walked into my father's rooms. He was sat on his marble chair, eyes guarded.

"Lucifer, you are my brightest child and yet you have proven to be the most defiant. Why have you chosen this path?"

As if he doesn't know the answer to that question. I've said it a thousand times.

"I want to be free."

"Freedom comes at a price, my son."

"Does their freedom come at a cost?"

Humans. The crux of our every argument. They are given the whole world to run riot in and yet we are stuck in servitude to them day after day.

"It will. Someone has to punish those who have trespassed against their fellow men and women. Those who have sinned."

I watched him carefully for signs of what he could possibly mean by that. Punishment. He can create someone to carry out this task, surely?

"*Azrael will be tested. He will come to hate humanity, but one day, he will learn his place and what his duty really means. A Darkness will come. One that will consume the world. Only he will be able to save them. And you will be there to make sure he follows through. It will come at a time and in a form neither of you will expect.*"

A Darkness? What kind of Darkness does he mean? Consuming the world?

"*It will be my wrath, Lucifer. If he does not save them, then all Heaven and Earth will burn. There is another place. A place for the souls of sinners. I will call it Hell. And you will be its King.*"

I stared at him. Hell? King?

"*You would have me punish sinners?*"

"*You are a disappointment, Lucifer. You have always been my favourite and yet, you have the strongest will. Unbreakable. Is it not fitting that you should break those who have disappointed me? Those who have hurt, maimed and killed?*"

I took a step back, seeing my entire existence in Heaven flash before my eyes in an instant. All of it gone. Wasted.

"*You will never return to Heaven. Eternity, Lucifer. You are consigned to Hell for eternity.*"

Before I had a chance to speak, the room spun around. I stood before the gates of Heaven with Azrael next to me. Our father stood just inside them, his expression sorrowful.

"*My sons, you are to be exiled from Heaven. Never shall you cross these gates. Never shall you infect the minds of your fellow angels with lies and deceit. You wanted freedom. You're free to roam Earth as you please, but do not forget your duty, Lucifer. Do not forget you owe your life to Hell.*"

He put his hands out. I felt myself falling, falling and I could not beat my wings to fly back up. They burnt with an intensity I'd never experienced before.

Where was Azrael? I can't see him. My vision went dark around the edges.

I landed with a thump. When I opened my eyes, I found myself surrounded by blackened earth. Rising to my feet, I looked around.

All I could see is fire.

The fire which never dies.

And I know.

I am in Hell.

કે ન્છ

Lucifer felt dampness on his hand, pulling it away, he found Candace's face wet with tears. He hadn't noticed, so lost in the day the Devil was born.

She opened her eyes, staring up at him.

"I had no idea," she whispered. "I should never have asked you to tell me."

She reached up, holding his face and pressing her forehead to his.

"Humans think their God is benevolent. To them, perhaps, but to His angels, never. Especially not to the one He called His favourite son."

"He was right about one thing... You are unbreakable."

He laughed. It was hollow.

"Perhaps that was true before, but not now. You see, I gave my soul to a witch and if she leaves me, I'll break and the pieces of my soul will scatter in the wind."

Her bottom lip trembled. A sob escaped her perfect mouth. He cupped her cheek, knowing she wasn't able to speak at that moment.

"Shh, don't cry any more for me." He wiped her cheek with his thumb. "Showing you my worst memory was not meant to upset you. I trust you, little witch, with everything. I want you to remember that when you're afraid."

She pressed her mouth to his. Her lips were damp from her tears.

"*Thank you for trusting me. I won't be afraid any more. Next week, I'll tell my mother then we'll have forever.*"

If only that were true. They would have years, but forever wasn't on the cards. Not when he knew her soul belonged in Heaven.

Chapter Twenty Seven

*L*ucifer watched her hands shaking as they walked down the long corridor. The double doors at the end were dark wood with intricate carvings of the fae. Beyond lay her mother's dining room.

"I don't want to do this," she whispered.

He put a hand on her arm.

"I'm here, little witch. You need not be afraid."

She looked at him, violet eyes betraying her inner turmoil.

"I don't want to pretend. She'll have invited the royal families. I can't stand any of them. Stuck up wastes of space. They think I'm polite, courteous and obedient. I never gave them any reason to think otherwise."

"Then they'll just have to learn who their princess truly is."

She half smiled at him, turning back to the doors. They opened as they drew closer. Most of the seats were already filled. Her mother sat at the very head of the table. The laughter and voices rang through the room as they neared the doors.

And then, everything froze. Lucifer stopped, the hairs on the back of his neck pricking up. He eyed Candace, but she'd been frozen in place too. There could only be one explanation.

"Father."

"Hello Lucifer."

He stiffened.

What the fuck is He doing here? Of all the times He could have come, why now?

"I am here because the time has come for you to learn your final lesson."

He'd forgotten he couldn't hide anything from his father. It had been so long since he'd heard the Divine's voice. So long since he'd been in his presence, he'd forgotten what it felt like.

"And what lesson would that be?"

Fuck His lessons. It's just another way to punish me for my inability to be His perfect son.

"I'm going to give you a choice. Either way, you will have to sacrifice something you care about."

Candace.

His heart constricted painfully. Anger blazed in his veins. His father using the woman he loved against him was a whole new low.

"She has always been the one you must sacrifice."

"Haven't you done enough? Do you want me to break, Father? The son you called strong willed and unbreakable now has a weakness and you clearly intend to exploit it. Your cruelty knows no bounds."

His father said nothing in response.

Sacrifice. Sacrifice.

The realisation dawned on him like a ton of bricks slamming down on his heart.

"She who is born under the two stars. She who belongs to two worlds. She who comes to you in darkness. She who comes to you in light. She will bring the dawn and cast out the night. She will restore you. She will be your sacrifice."

The air around him seemed to drop a few degrees. The lights flickered.

That idiotic prophecy. Why am I not surprised? I should've known it was about us.

Darkness. Light. Dawn. Devil. Light bringer. Morningstar. The references were clear as day now.

"It is your choice, Lucifer. Is she really worthy of you?"

"Of course she's fucking worthy. It's me who's not worthy of her."

"You would place a half witch, half fae girl above yourself? That is... unexpected."

He rarely surprised his father. He supposed this was a change in pace.

"If you'd bothered to look in my head, you'd know why. I love her."

"The last time we spoke, you hated mortals. Tell me. What changed?"

Everything. She changed everything. And I don't hate her for it. I always needed her. She fills the void in my soul.

"I don't need to tell you anything. What is this choice you wish me to make?"

His father sighed deeply. Lucifer didn't turn around to look at him. He had no wish to see the one who'd taken everything from him.

"That girl is more powerful than she realises. If she is truly worthy of being your queen, then she must prove it. She stands at a crossroads. She can turn her back on her people and live a lifetime with you before I take her soul to Heaven. The second option requires her to take a life. Her mother's in exchange for eternity. To live and rule by your side, she must commit a mortal sin. The choice is yours."

He almost fell to his knees at his father's pronouncement.

He expects her to damn herself to prove she's worthy of me? What the fuck kind of sick joke is this? How can He ask me to decide? How can I ever force her to kill her own mother to be with me forever?

"You're sick, you know that, right? After you forced Azrael to murder the woman he loves I thought you'd be done with punishing us. Clearly, I was wrong."

"This isn't a punishment."

"It fucking feels like one."

His heart broke. This wasn't a decision he could make. And there was one very important thing she didn't know.

"Let me talk to her."

"No."

"Let me speak to her. I won't tell her what you've said. I just need a moment with her, please."

If He's going to make me go through with this, it's the least He can fucking do.

Why did his father always have to make things so difficult? He'd taken Azrael's warning about God being restless seriously. This was why. He was sure of it.

"If you attempt to tell her about it, I will take away your choices."

"I'm not stupid," Lucifer muttered.

Candace unfroze, blinking rapidly. Her eyes went wide. He turned to her, taking her hand in his.

"What's happening? Why is... Are they frozen? What's going on?" she said.

"Shh, look at me, little witch."

She turned to him, confusion in her expression. His heart lurched.

"Why are they frozen?"

"It doesn't matter, I need you to listen to me carefully."

He let go of her hand, cupping both her cheeks.

She's so beautiful, so pure, so perfect. How can I ask her to damn her soul for me? How can He ask me to make this choice on her behalf?

"Do you love me?" he asked.

"You know I do. What is this about?"

"Just listen and answer my questions."

"Lucifer, you're scaring me. Why is everything frozen except us?"

See what you've done, Father? She's not ready for any of this. Fuck.

He didn't want to make this choice. She should decide. This was her life and her soul on the line.

"I'm sorry, please don't be afraid. You said you wanted forever with me. How much would you give up for that?"

"Everything."

There was no hesitation in her voice.

Fuck. She has no idea what that really means.

"Little witch, are you sure you wish for eternity in Hell with me? Am I really worth giving up your entire life for?"

Her violet eyes widened.

"Why are you asking me this? I thought it's what you wanted. You told me you couldn't live without me."

"Please, just humour me for a moment."

His father had so many things to answer for. This most of all. He couldn't come out and tell her why he needed to know. He just had to be sure of her answer. Sure of her resolve.

"You are worth sacrificing everything for, Lucifer. You know how I feel. I love you. My soul is yours. I am yours."

Her soul.

She'd given it to him. That's why his father was forcing him to decide. He knew what he had to do. He pulled her closer, pressing his mouth to hers. She kissed him back, wrapping her arms around his waist.

Please don't hate me.

"How could I ever? You're everything. Nothing you've done or will do can change that."

When he pulled away, he rested his forehead against hers, staring down into her violet eyes.

"Promise me you'll do what's necessary, little witch. Do what you need to survive. Show me how much you love me."

"I promise even though I don't know why you're being like this."

"Lucifer, it's time," his father said.

He stiffened. There was only one thing left to say and he had to do it now.

"Little witch... Candace..."

"What is it?" she asked.

"There's one thing you should know before you go in there."

She blinked, her lip twitching.

"I love you."

There was a moment of silence. Her eyes fixed on his.

"You what?" she whispered.

"I love you, my little witch. I always will."

Tears pricked at her eyes.

"Shh, don't cry," he said.

"You... you love me."

"Yes."

Her hands came up, capturing his face before she kissed him. There had been no reason to keep her in the dark any longer. She needed to know before she went in there and changed her life forever. He'd made a decision. He could only hope she kept her resolve never to hate him for anything he did.

I love her and she loves me. That has to be enough.

"I grow weary of your stalling, Lucifer," his father said.

Lucifer pulled away from Candace.

"It'll be okay, little witch, I promise," he whispered.

She nodded, staring up at him with adoration on her face.

Fuck. I hope you still look at me in the same way when this is done.

"Have you decided?" his father asked.

"Yes. Don't make me say it."

"Who are you talking to?" Candace said.

"It doesn't matter. Remember I love you. Remember that when everything seems dark, okay?"

She nodded again.

Just do it, Father. You know my answer.

"Let go of her. She has to do this alone. You cannot help her," his father replied.

Lucifer kissed her forehead before stepping away.

"You're strong enough, Candace. I trust you. Do this for us."

He knew she wouldn't know what he was talking about, but he had to say it anyway.

"Are you not coming with me?" she asked.

He shook his head. It wouldn't do for him to be visible to her mother. She knew that.

"I'll be here for you, but we talked about this. It'll only make it worse for you if she sees me."

She looked at her feet, wringing her hands.

"I know."

The sounds from the fae filtered through to them and he knew God had restarted time.

Candace gave him one last significant look before she strode into her mother's dining room. He trailed along behind, standing just inside the doors before they closed.

No one but his little witch knew he was there. If he interfered in anyway, then all would be lost. His heart lurched.

Little witch, you can do this. I know you can. I know you.

❧　❧

Candace curtsied to her mother before her chair was pulled out and she sat down. The queen looked over her outfit with approval.

Well, at least I've not disappointed her yet.

She wore a long, dark green dress with gold embellishments. Mall had helped her pick it out when they'd returned to Hell for a few days. Her heart contracted.

Lucifer.

He'd been acting strangely before they'd come in and she had no idea how time had suddenly been frozen. It was best not to think about it. He'd told her it didn't matter.

"It's nice of you to join us," her mother said.

Candace kept a straight face.

Can't rock the boat just yet even if she's being a sarcastic bitch right now.

"I apologise, Mother."

"Cadmi, it has been an age," said a deep voice to her right.

Candace turned at the sound, seated next to her was Theodus' father, Prince Mitah Farlane. She really couldn't stand him.

"Yes, it is a shame you were not able to attend the ball. How are your other children?"

"They are well, thank you. Novus has just returned from Europe."

She drowned out his chatter, nodding at him at appropriate moments. Her eyes drifted over to the doors where Lucifer stood. He looked tense. She knew only she could see him, so she didn't allow her gaze to linger. Knowing he was there made this a little easier.

"Candace," her mother hissed.

She leant a little closer to Gwilliana, wondering what on earth she wanted.

"Why have you not said hello to Theodus?"

As if I want to say hello to that prick.

She half smiled at him from across the table, giving a little nod. He smiled in return, but it didn't meet his eyes.

"Happy now?" Candace hissed back.

"No. What is wrong with the two of you?"

"Wrong? Nothing."

"Do not lie to me."

She wants to do this now? Fine. I don't want to be here any longer anyway. This is what I came here to do. I need to end this ridiculous sham.

"What's wrong is he's a prick and I'm not marrying him."

Gwilliana's eyes flashed with anger.

"Are you trying to test me?"

Candace took a breath.

Now or never.

There was never a more perfect moment to tell her mother exactly how she felt.

"No, that's the truth. I came here today to tell you the engagement is off. I'm going to spend my life with the man I love, not with someone you chose for me because you're obsessed with a stupid prophecy that isn't even about you."

She looked over at Lucifer again. She'd thought a lot about what the prophecy meant. Who it alluded to. Something clicked a few days ago when they'd been in Hell. Lucifer had been sprawled out on the sofa playing with a ball of light. Before he'd fallen, he'd been known as the Morningstar. She'd almost fallen off the stool when she'd realised.

"It's about me and him."

Chapter Twenty Eight

*L*ucifer stiffened at her words.

She knows. How long has she known it was about us? Does she know what she has to do?

Candace looked away from him, back to her mother. The queen's expression was thunderous.

"You dare say such things to me," Gwilliana seethed, no longer keeping her voice low.

The other fae at the table looked to their queen, frowns on their faces.

"I dare?" Candace replied, pushing her chair back and standing. "You're the one who's been lying to your court for centuries. You're perfectly capable of carrying children. I'm not your saviour, Mother, nor your sacrifice. I refuse to be a part of this any longer."

Gwilliana jumped to her feet, her eyes blazing with unconcealed fury. He saw the flash of magic in her hand before it flew at Candace. His witch blocked it with efficiency, creating a pink barrier around her which glittered with both witch and fae magic. She stepped backwards around her chair.

"You little bitch. I knew you were going to be trouble. You've always been your father's daughter."

"You want to know why that is? Because he raised me, not you. He taught me how to be a witch, not one of the fae. All you and your court have done is scorn me for being a half breed. No more. I'm more than just your little obedient daughter trapped by what she thought was her duty. I learnt a lesson when I was in Hell, Mother. A lesson about freedom and cages.

Freedom comes at a price and I much prefer to choose my own cage rather than be stuck in chains by you."

Her mother sent further spells against Candace's barrier, but they all bounced off harmlessly. The rest of the assembled fae looked shocked, but they didn't move to help either of them.

That idiot prince looks as though he's finally realised she's never going to be his. Serves him fucking right. She's mine and she always will be.

He wanted to go to her, but he held back.

"Tell me, daughter, how do you know the prophecy is not about the fae? Who is this he you speak of?"

"Do you really want to know? Are you sure you can handle the truth?"

Lucifer stiffened. If she told her mother, would he be able to stay hidden? Would she want him to reveal himself? He couldn't. His father would see it as interference.

"It seems your true colours are shining through, Candace. Might as well reveal all your secrets."

She didn't look his way. She wore a smirk, her eyes wild with amusement.

"Darkness and light, Mother. There is only one being in this world who personifies those two things equally. Only one who brought the dawn. He goes by many names, but you will only ever remember him as the one who set your daughter free."

Gwilliana staggered backwards, placing her hand on her heart. Her violet eyes went wide.

"You... you cannot possibly be serious?"

The rest of the fae looked at each other with confusion. Candace shook her head. He knew exactly what she was thinking.

Fools. They cannot see what's right in front of them.

"Tell them, Mother. Tell them who it is."

"Lucifer," her mother whispered.

He rolled his eyes at the collective gasp around the room.

Bunch of stuck up fuckwits. They probably think I'm evil and not to be trusted.

"That's right. The prophecy is about me and him, not you. It was never about you. I finally know that now. So, as I said to you earlier, I won't do what you say. I belong to him and no one else can have me."

She pulled up the hem of her dress, exposing her ankle. The blood drained from Gwilliana's face. No one spoke for a long moment. The queen's expression hardened as she continued to stare down at her daughter's ankle. Candace let her dress fall back. She looked so strong, so assured.

My little witch, you might have defied your mother, but this isn't over. I hope you know that.

"You don't deserve to be called my daughter," Gwilliana seethed.

Her mother struck, her magic flaring out and breaking through Candace's barrier. Candace put a hand up, pink smoke flaring out and stopping her mother's spell in its tracks. Her expression darkened. He noticed a change within her immediately. Little flecks of pink glitter swirled within the smoke.

Her magic has fused. The two sides of her. Fuck. He was right. She is more powerful than she realises.

"You'd rather kill me than live knowing your daughter is in love with the Devil?" Candace asked, anger in her eyes.

"You're sick, daughter. Sick. Allowing such evil to seep into your heart."

"Evil? The only evil in this room is you. Too long have you kept everyone under your sway. You know nothing."

"And you deserve nothing."

The next moment happened so fast, no one moved for a long moment when it was done. Both women had cast a spell, but only one found its mark. Gwilliana looked down at the patch of her dress where her heart lay. It was rapidly darkening, stained with blood. She looked back up at Candace. His little witch stared at her mother without any visible emotion on her face.

"You... you..." Gwilliana said before she collapsed to her knees, clutching her chest.

"Goodbye Mother."

Candace turned on her heel and strode towards the doors. The attendants pulled them open and she walked out, leaving the fae to stare at their dying queen. Lucifer stood for a moment, unable to quite comprehend the turn of events.

What will she say when she discovers I decided she had to kill her mother? I have to tell her. Now.

Gwilliana took her last breath and collapsed in a heap on the floor. There was a scream from one of the fae women followed by a growl from a male.

Lucifer didn't stop to survey the damage inflicted any further, he turned away, chasing after his witch.

He caught up with her outside her mother's mansion. He put a hand on her arm, stopping her in her tracks. She turned to him, eyes full of tears.

"I killed her," she whispered. "I killed my own mother."

Fuck. How can I tell her when she looks like that? No, I have no choice.

He let her go, taking a step back.

"I'm sorry, little witch, this is my fault."

She frowned, tears rolling down her cheeks. She tried to reach for him, but he stepped away again. He needed to keep his resolve to tell her and he couldn't do that if she barrelled her way into his arms.

"What? You didn't make me kill my own mother."

"I... Candace, my Father was here. That's why time froze. He gave me a choice, to have you for a lifetime or to have you for eternity."

"He was here? Shit, I'm sorry. That must've been awful. Surely you chose for us to have eternity?"

He looked away. The affection she held in her eyes was completely undeserved. He wasn't worthy of her. Not after the choice he'd made.

I've been so fucking selfish.

"Eternity came at a price, little witch. The price was to damn your soul. You had to take a life. Her life. To prove yourself worthy of me. He demanded I decide and if I told you, He would've taken away any choice. I'm sorry."

The moments of silence and stillness unnerved him, but he didn't look at her.

What if she hates me? I know she said she wouldn't but how can she not?

He felt a hand under his chin. She turned his face back towards her. When he took in her expression, his heart thumped in his chest. Her tears had stopped, but she didn't look at him in anger. Love radiated from her.

"Lucifer, you showed me how cruel He could be when you gave me the gift of your worst memory." She put a hand on his heart. "I love you. I told you, nothing you do will change that fact. You've given us forever. If I hadn't killed her, she'd have killed me. That's what her spell was. I just turned it back against her. I don't care that I've damned my soul. If that's His price, then fucking so be it. I'm tired of expectations and duties. All I want is you and me. It's done now, isn't it?"

"Yes."

"Then neither of us can change it. I know why you chose it."

She cupped his face, pulling him down towards her. When their lips met, he groaned, tugging her into his arms. She pressed herself closer, her hands curling around his neck, fingers in his hair.

I love you, little witch. I love you forever.

"I love you too, my beautiful dark angel."

When they released each other, they both smiled. He wiped away her lingering tears.

"Should we return home?" he asked.

"I need to do something first. Just one thing then I promise we can go home."

She went up on her tiptoes and whispered it in his ear. He picked her up and they took to the skies.

☙ ❧

He placed her gently down on the ground outside a house in a quiet street. She kissed his cheek and walked up to the door, pressing down on the bell.

A few minutes later, it opened, revealing a blonde girl with green eyes.

"Oh, hi," the girl said.

"Is he here?" Candace asked.

"Um, yes... I didn't expect to see you. He told me you were fighting."

"We were. Look, I just need a minute with him, Sam."

Sam turned, shouting Jaxon's name. He walked out a moment later, stopping dead when he spied Candace with Lucifer standing a few feet behind her.

"Jax, I don't want you to say anything. I just want you to know I forgive you. Whatever has happened in the past can stay there. I didn't want to leave with there being bad blood between us. You'll always be my best friend."

Jax was silent for a moment before he stepped out and wrapped his arms around Candace. Lucifer stiffened, holding back a growl.

I still don't trust that boy, but this is for her.

"I'm sorry, Cadmi," Jax whispered. "I just want you to be happy."

"I know." She stepped back from his embrace. "I'll see you soon, okay?"

He nodded. She turned away from him and walked back to Lucifer.

"I'm ready," she said.

He picked her up, his wings flaring out. Sam let out an audible gasp.

"Who's that?" she hissed at Jax.

"Lucifer, Cadmi's lover."

"What?"

"I'll tell you about it in the house, come on."

Lucifer took to the skies, smiling. They landed in Hyde Park and were through the portal half an hour later. He didn't put her down, taking her straight into their bedroom. He placed her on the bed, crawling over her with a grin on his face.

"What are you so happy about?" she asked, brushing a lock of hair from his face.

"My queen is finally home with me."

"Are you suddenly turning soppy on me?"

He frowned, growling a little. He took her wrists and pinned them above her head.

"No. Do you need me to teach you a lesson, little witch?"

She smiled at him, shaking her head.

"No, but I do need to speak to my dad."

He released her, sitting up on his knees between her legs. She pulled her phone off the bedside table where she'd left it earlier and dialled. He'd modified it for her so she could speak to those on Earth she cared for.

"Hello Candace," her father said when he answered.

Lucifer shifted back, capturing each of her legs and tugging off her shoes.

"Dad, I need to tell you something."

"I already know, my child."

Lucifer trailed his fingers up her calves, earning a hard stare from his little witch. He grinned, the smile wicked.

"You do?"

"You know the fae speak to their loved one for one last time before their soul fades."

"She came to you? That's... oh."

Lucifer pushed up her dress, hooking his fingers into her underwear and tugging them off. She looked at him but didn't comment.

"She's sorry it happened that way. Her anger for you faded the moment she realised what she'd truly done. It's okay, I know it was her or you."

"It was. She went mental at me after I told her I wasn't going to do her bidding. Perhaps I shouldn't have provoked her with the prophecy and who it's really about."

Her dress bunched up around her waist. He leant down, kissing her inner thighs. She let out an almost inaudible gasp but didn't stop him.

"You worked it out then. I knew you would eventually. I hope you and he are happy together. I love you."

"We will be, love you too, Dad. Why did she appear to you?"

He buried his face in her softness, tongue lashing out against her core. She bucked her hips.

"I think your mother always regretted the way she left things between us. She often told me I was her greatest love, though she had many men before me. Perhaps that's why. I think my love for her faded when I realised how little she cared about your happiness. I still cared for her though. She gave me you."

Lucifer put his hand on her stomach, keeping her pinned to the bed as he continued to pleasure her.

Little witch, you're mine. The taste of her is intoxicating.

"I don't... hate her. I don't feel so great about what I did, but she left me no choice."

Her hand tangled in his hair, clutching his scalp.

She wants me to stop, but I can't. I need her. Fuck do I need her. I'm going to fuck her when she's off the phone.

After everything that had occurred, all he wanted was to remind them both of what they fought for.

Each other.

"I know she didn't."

"I... uh, Dad, I have to go now."

"Okay, Candace. Keep in touch."

"I will."

She hung up, throwing the phone away and groaning.

"Lucifer, that's not fair."

He chuckled, raising his head.

"I told you, all's fair in love and war."

She raised an eyebrow, pointing at him.

"You're a very bad angel."

"Mmm, I just wish to make love to my queen."

"Is that so?"

"I intend to make love to her for eternity." He moved, crawling over her. "I also intend to fuck her, break her and ruin her over and over again."

"And punish her?"

"Mmm, yes, that too."

She tugged him towards her by his hair.

"Then make good on those intentions now before I combust on the spot."

He grinned, kissing her. He took her hands, pinning them to the bed again. She wrapped a leg around his waist, holding him to her.

"I love you forever."

And I love you for eternity, my little witch.

Acknowledgements

Thank you for reading this book. As an indie author, reviews are very important to me. I hope you consider leaving one if you enjoyed it.
Lucifer's Cage came to me right before I finished Death's Angel. This was the one I wasn't meant to write, but Lucifer had other ideas. When I introduced him into the After Dark universe, I wasn't expecting him to be such an interesting, dark and complex character. Writing him was an absolute joy.

When I set out to write this book, I decided it was going to mix things up. The first five books were about girls who'd never been introduced to the supernatural. I wanted to be able to explore factions between communities from the point of view of those who'd grown up in it. And if I was going to write Lucifer a love interest, she had to be special, unique and able to call him out on his bullshit. When Candace, a half witch, half fae came along, I knew she was perfect. The two of them were electric together. She came alive on the page in a way I hadn't expected and I love her all the more for it.

I think the hardest challenge for me was writing the fall from Heaven scene. It's such an iconic moment and I really needed it to have the right impact. It showed so much vulnerability. The version of Lucifer before the Fall differed greatly from the archangel we see now. My Lucifer was never going to be evil. Sinful perhaps, but there's so much more to him. Bringing out those sides to him in this book gave me such a complex array of emotions. I felt Lucifer's pleasure and his pain as I wrote his words.

I'm aware I pushed the boundaries in Death's Angel, but Lucifer's Cage took things to a whole new level. It is the steamiest book in the After Dark universe and I make absolutely no apologies for that. Lucifer was never going to do vanilla. An archangel who'd fallen and ruled Hell. As if vanilla would ever be satisfying for such a man. The chemistry between the two of them was always going to be explosive and I enjoyed bringing that to the forefront.

And of course, lastly, I'm really looking forward to bringing you the next book in the series. I couldn't leave the story of what happens now the fae queen is dead untold. The ripple effect in the universe is always far reaching.

I'd firstly like to thank my wonderful readers for joining me on this journey. I wouldn't still be writing this series if it wasn't for you and I hope this was just as satisfying for you as the previous books.

I need to say a huge thank you to my best friend and fellow author, Sab. You are my hero and my twin. When I told her, I was writing Lucifer's story, she was so excited. That's when I knew it was the right decision to continue the series. How could I not when my bestie was desperate for his story? She's been with me every step of the way since the release of Demon's Destiny and I could not ask for more.

My next huge thank you goes to Sean McMahon – the wonderful author of the Restarter series. He has been a constant source of support and love. Getting to meet him in person was an amazing experience. He's there when I need him and always willing to offer advice. Having a fellow indie author who understands all the struggles is a blessing.

And last, but not least, thank you to my husband for putting up with me. You know I wouldn't be doing any of this without you. I love you to the stars and back.

About the Author

Born and raised in Sussex, UK near the Ashdown Forest where she grew up climbing trees and building Lego towns with her younger brother. Sarah fell in love with novels when she was a teenager reading her aunt's historical regency romances. She has always loved the supernatural and exploring the darker side of romance and fantasy novels.

Sarah currently resides in the Scottish Highlands with her husband. Music is one of her biggest inspirations and she always has something on in the background whilst writing. She is an avid gamer and is often found hogging her husband's Xbox.

Sign up to her mailing list to find out about her latest releases, promotions and giveaways below:
www.subscribepage.com/sarahbaileywriter

You can find more about Sarah Bailey in the following ways:
www.sarahbaileywriter.com
www.facebook.com/sbaileyauthor
www.twitter.com/sbaileyauthor
www.instagram.com/sbaileyauthor

The Sequel to Lucifer's Cage

Blood Magic

A forbidden friendship. Two worlds colliding. Blood and magic.

When Jamie returns to London at the behest of his older sibling, he does not expect to run into a princess, let alone the youngest daughter of the newly crowned King of the Fae. The innocent Dani is looking for excitement, fun and a little darkness. The sinful Jamie cannot resist the call. The problem? Gavin doesn't want him anywhere near Dani. Not when there is unrest in both the vampire and the fae communities.

As Jamie and Dani form a fast friendship, one fateful night changes everything. Dani is caught between loyalty to her people and her relationship with the playful, flirtatious vampire. And Jamie isn't about to let the fae girl who sets his world ablaze out of his sights.

How far are they willing to go for each other? And what happens when Gavin and King Mitah discover the forbidden friendship between the princess and the vampire?

Made in the USA
San Bernardino, CA
11 February 2019